CW01394893

BEOW'ULF
REVELATIONS

THE FORGOTTEN
ANGLO-SAXON KING

George W Jones

Published by Country Books
an imprint of
Spiral Publishing Ltd

Country Books, 38 Pulla Hill Drive,
Storrington, West Sussex RH20 3LS

email: jonathan@spiralpublishing.com
www.spiral-books.com

ISBN 978-1-0685670-2-5

© 2025 George William Jones

The rights of George William Jones have been asserted in
accordance with the Copyright, Designs and Patents Act 1993.

All rights reserved. No part of this publication may be reproduced,
stored in a retrieval system, or transmitted, in any way or form, or
by any means, electronic, mechanical, photocopying, or otherwise,
without the prior permission of the author and publisher.

British Library Cataloguing in Publication Data.
A catalogue record for this book is available from the
British Library.

Printed and bound in England by 4edge Limited,
22 Eldon Way Industrial Estate, Hockley, Essex SS5 4AD

TRANSLATION LICENCES

JRR TOLKIEN

Reprinted by permission of Harper Collins Publishers Limited
© 2024 George William Jones
Licence: HC 2024-0055030

RD FULK

Reprinted by permission of Harvard University Press
© 2024 George William Jones
Licence: R-12216

SEAMUS HEANEY

Reprinted by permission of FABER AND FABER Limited
© 2024 George William Jones
Licence: P231231/117

Beowulf Artwork
by HJ Ford

H.J. Ford
Wikipedia

Henry Justice Ford (1860–1941) was a prolific and successful English artist and illustrator, active from 1886 through to the late 1920s. Sometimes known as H. J. Ford or Henry J. Ford, he came to public attention when he provided the numerous beautiful illustrations for Andrew Lang's Fairy Books, which captured the imagination of a generation of British children and were sold worldwide in the 1880s and 1890s.

"When you have eliminated the impossible, whatever remains, however improbable, must be the truth."

Arthur Conan Doyle

Peacehaven
Beowulf's Barrow
Kingston
Swanborough
Iford
Newhaven
Piddinghoe
Southease
Rodmell
Tarring Neville
WALLANDS PARK
Offham
Lewes
Hamsey
Cooksbridge
Old St Peter's Church, Hamsey
Bishopstone
Malling Hill
SOUTH MALLING
Beddingham
Mount Caburn
Barcombe
Ringmer
Gote Lane
Middleham
Glynde
West Firle
West Firle
GLYNDEBOURNE
Glyndebourne
Ringmer
Image © 2024 Airbus
Old Hag Woods
Holt Hill
Google Earth

CONTENTS

CONTENTS

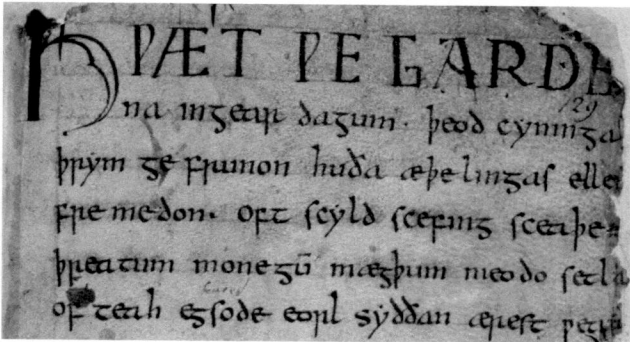

INTRODUCTION

"So. The Spear-Danes in days gone by and the kings who ruled them had courage and greatness. We have heard of those princes' heroic campaigns."

(Opening Lines)
The Beowulf Manuscript
Seamus Heaney Translation

The *Beowulf Manuscript* is an intriguing ancient document. The sole surviving copy which is now housed in the British Library has been studied and translated by many writers and historians, including the literary giants JRR Tolkien and Seamus Heaney. Lacking the research tools of the modern day and any further evidence to work from, these accomplished academics have all been left to wonder whether the *Beowulf* text is based on fact or fiction. Some have insisted that it is a tale from the realms of myth, others have noted the many corresponding characters from history and have deemed it to be true; most have concluded that the answer must lie somewhere in between. It is my hope that this book will finally unravel this confusing mystery.

Incredibly, the story of *Beowulf* appears to be largely based within historical and geographical fact, but crucially, it is also a projection from the eyes, mind and time of the man who wrote it. The events described in the text are far more accurate than you would ever believe. As this research reflects, *Beowulf* also appears to be a story that is connected to many early Anglo-Saxon kings, all of whom we will find in the historical records of Wessex, Mercia, and East Anglia.

Astonishingly, it would also appear that a real-life "dragon" (of a sort) really did exist in Sussex during the time of the Anglo-Saxons, but its species lives on to this day in the realms of a world where it does not possess an ability to fly or to breathe fire, and yet, both flying dragons and fire were certainly witnessed by the Anglo-Saxons of the time. The monster, Grendel, who Beowulf wrestles with at the great hall called Heorot, is, in all likelihood, the common monster of a man.

In this research-oriented book, we will cover all of these subjects in detail and discover a solid premise for the precise location of Beowulf's dramatic death scene. Additionally, we will uncover a highly probable site for his burial mound and a museum where his burned bones and funerary urn may now rest, unknown to the curators; this may also lead us to discover where his priceless grave goods may have gone.

Throughout this book, we will begin to unravel historical secrets and mysteries that have confounded researchers for decades. It is now my great pleasure to attempt to explain the reality behind this remarkable story in the most effective way that I can. I hope that you find these verifiable connections to this wonderful epic as fascinating and exciting as I have. Once this literary jigsaw is complete, we will be left with a new picture of *Beowulf* that may also help us to reshape some of the early history of Anglo-Saxon England as we currently know it.

A brief note on the layout and techniques used within this research...

With so many spurious claims, studies and assertions put forward in the modern day, I have decided that quoting crucial references will be far more helpful to us here than simply referencing the references; we can then confirm their meaning immediately, without the reader having to simply take my word for it. As there are so many critical and intricate details to cover, I feel this will provide us with an effective method to confirm the truth of these research-related, literary and historical associations. I have also included many pictures in this production to show you precisely what I am referring to in each scenario. The adage, "a picture paints a thousand words," is still true today and is a resource I have attempted to utilise here where words cannot do justice to the findings on their own. The critical tool of etymology is a further key I have purposed for many of my discoveries. In plain sight yet hidden away in the very origins of our everyday words, in place names, and even in people's names, are numerous secrets for us to examine that speak of the very beginnings of our original written history. Some initial, worthwhile examples of etymology can be found in the origins of the names for the seven days of the week, all attributed to various deities of the past...

Monday ~ Moon Day
Tuesday ~ Tiw's Day
Wednesday ~ Woden's Day
Thursday ~ Thor's Day
Friday ~ Freya's Day
Saturday ~ Saturn's Day
Sunday ~ Sun's Day

Whilst admittedly, we cannot rely solely on etymology to give us a truly accurate reflection of past events, the deeper meanings that can be found within the origins of *all* words and names often prove to be most enlightening. When examined in detail, etymology allows us a brief, informative glimpse into the past. Combining this information with historical records and focused observation of geography, we can build the largest picture available to us, which can then help us build an enormous jigsaw puzzle with all of the pieces taken into consideration.

Regarding the use of this method, it is important that we do not choose to "throw the baby out with the bath water." If we take the *Anglo-Saxon Chronicle* as an example, should we only consider certain information contained within the text to be true and the rest of it false, or should we look at all of it with an open mind? A fantastic example to consider in relation to this scenario is the mention of serpents and dragons seen in Sussex and England within the text of the *Anglo-Saxon Chronicle*. Should we believe that the scribe who recorded these events simply had a mental break and only imagined them, or is there a logical explanation that can be found if we choose to examine all of the information available to us with a keen eye on the details? If we consider that most of our knowledge concerning the Anglo-Saxon period comes directly from this one source, should we subsequently dismiss *all* of it as fiction because it mentions something that we cannot comprehend? I do not believe so, but if we want to discover the truth behind these curious entries, we are forced to take serious note of them and then dig very deep and in various directions to find the answers. In doing so, we can discover some remarkable clues to some baffling questions, including a highly probable solution to the dragon and serpents in Sussex riddle, which links directly into the *Beowulf* story.

One further source I have utilised here is moderately contentious, but in relation to the information I will be presenting, it has proved to be particularly useful. Wikipedia is an online encyclopaedia that can often prove somewhat biased concerning some subject matter. However, the entries that I will be presenting from the site have all been checked for accuracy and concern verifiable historical information that has often been compiled into a helpful paragraph or two from various recorded references. This allows us to glean essential information without the need to read multiple books for the same result. As with all modern media, we should be careful not to believe everything we are presented with from any source. Checking the facts behind any bold claim is always worthwhile.

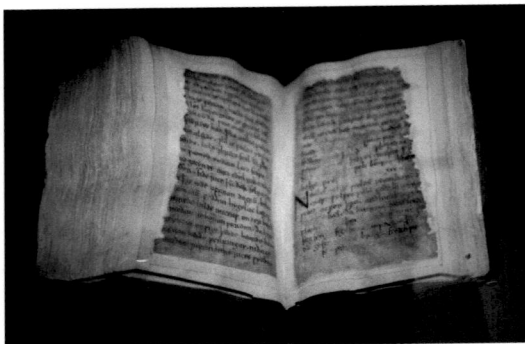

~ CHAPTER 1 ~

THE BEOWULF MANUSCRIPT

I t would be helpful, but not essential, for any reader of this research to have some cursory knowledge of the story of *Beowulf*. For those who do not, I would like to begin by briefly introducing you to the background of the manuscript, what it consists of, and where it was found.

Beowulf is the modern given name for the only surviving copy of an untitled collection of manuscripts (now called the *Nowell Codex*), discovered in a library at a property called Ashburnham House, which ironically (ash-burn-ham) burnt down in a raging fire in the year 1731. Sadly, that terrible fire struck hard at the home's precious library, consuming many priceless works of literature. To our great detriment, it seems likely that many other versions of the critically important *Anglo-Saxon Chronicle* were lost in the blaze. Incredibly though, the compilation of manuscripts that included the story of

Beowulf was saved and preserved, singed around the edges but remaining largely legible with the loss of only a few words on the outer edge of the pages. Thankfully, *Beowulf* survived by a whisker and captured the imaginations of countless minds to follow.

It has been proposed by researchers that the events of the story occurred between 500 and 900 AD. The manuscript itself dates to between 975 – 1025 AD. This precious book is now one of the earliest and most important works of Old English literature that has survived to the present day.

The first lines of the *Beowulf Manuscript* were examined and transcribed in 1705. Since then, scores of academics have attempted to translate the text, imparting a slight sense of themselves into each iteration. We find ourselves now, in the year 2024, with a vast array of differing versions to draw from. In the case of Seamus Heaney, we have a beautiful poetic rendition that stirs the imagination. In the case of JRR Tolkien, we are given a wonderfully considered translation emphasising accuracy and flow; in the case of RD Fulk, a more literal but equally well-composed translation. There are countless others, each with their own merits and drawbacks. As I have been learning from and utilising many versions, it has been fascinating to note the minor but critical differences of interpretation in each instance. We will discover many as we proceed.

The story itself primarily concerns the adventures of the legendary figure, Beowulf. His exploits in the epic tale include a battle with sea monsters and a journey across the ocean to face a beast-like man called Grendel, who has been laying waste to the lands and people of Hrothgar. After a heroic battle with Grendel and Grendel's mother, we follow Beowulf's journey home to Geatland. Decades later, in his old age, he has a fierce battle with a dragon that is guarding a hoard of treasure in a secret barrow underground. The tale ends with beautifully descriptive details concerning his funeral pyre and burial mound.

This brief introduction is an incredibly simplified version of the story that is suitable for our needs at this stage; however, the true scope of the text is quite extraordinary. We are provided with detailed descriptions of people and places, further references describing the decorations adorning the warriors' armour, and unfathomable lineages for the various tribes of the time. There are highly notable, wondrous intricacies in the vast scope of the story that most people today are largely unaware of. *Beowulf* is not a simple children's story or a work of fantasy. The level of attention to detail that this early author has presented us with is, in itself, a noteworthy clue to the basis of the text being found in historical fact. It would seem wholly unnecessary, during the time of the Anglo-Saxon's earliest written literature, to include these incredibly intricate details.

This astonishing and complex text is a hugely influential tale. It has seeded the foundations for some of the greatest heroic stories of our time, with *The Lord of the Rings* being a notable example. It is clearly observable that JRR Tolkien was not only an excellent Anglo-Saxon scholar but that he also drew much of his inspiration from the language and story of *Beowulf,* and then used it in the creation of *The Hobbit* and *The Lord of The Rings*. We will cover many of these parallels here as they become relevant.

The purpose of this book (as opposed to translating the Beowulf text again) is to transform the details of the story into as verifiable a real-world possibility as can be achieved and to examine some incredible parallels that are found in the reality of the historical, etymological, and geographical records of Sussex. From this new understanding, we can then begin to comprehend how a little-known historical figure appears to have seeded a legend that has now been transformed into one of the greatest surviving stories of all time. It has taken five years of detailed study, incredible luck, and deeply considered research to piece this story together. I hope the results speak clearly for themselves.

~ CHAPTER 2 ~

METAL DETECTING

***Sad at heart, addressing his companions,
Wiglaf spoke wise and fluent words:***

***"I remember that time when mead was flowing, how we
pledged loyalty to our lord in the hall, promised our ring
giver we would be worth our price, make good the gift
of the war gear, these swords and helmets, as and
when his need required it."***

(Wiglaf speaks of Beowulf)
The Beowulf Manuscript
Seamus Heaney Translation

To begin this investigation with some context, I would first like to explain how and why I began researching the *Beowulf Manuscript* in the first place...

This strange story of discovery began in late 2018 when I finally decided to do something I had always wanted to try: metal detecting. Having purchased a mid-range metal detector, a spade, and a finds pouch, I set out to find a piece of land I could get permission to dig on. My attention was first drawn to a piece of farmland that I had passed by thousands of times on my way to work, adjacent to Earwig Corner at the foot of Lewes in East Sussex, so I decided to see if there was any way I would be allowed to access it.

It seemed unlikely that I would be allowed to go there, but I drove to the farm and approached the farm manager to find out. Within moments, the farm owner arrived, and much to my surprise, he quickly and kindly agreed to let me detect there. I could not believe my luck. On my first land permission request, I had secured the exact field I was hoping to detect in. We agreed on a day for me to come back, and a couple of weeks later, filled with optimism and happy to finally be doing something I had always wanted to try, I walked up to the large sloping field from the farmyard across a network of horse pens and arrived at my destination.

Once I had made a considered, yet in the end, completely random choice for a place to begin, I turned on my detector, quickly got my first hit, and pulled up a shredded scrap of tin can. This was the first piece of metal-related rubbish that I dug up in that field, among hundreds of later pieces. I managed to fill entire bin bags over my many subsequent visits, but there was a good reason that I could not and would not give up. Hidden among the endless shards of litter, I had also found some incredibly beautiful, ancient Anglo-Saxon items that dated from the late 700s. The first little treasure to appear was an Anglo-Saxon zoomorphic strap end (a small piece of metal shaped like a little serpent that was once fixed to the end of a belt strap). The second item was an Anglo-Scandinavian bridle bit piece from a unique cavalry unit dated to the mid-700s, and the third item was an Anglo-Scandinavian stirrup strap mount from the same period. The feeling of holding something from over 1200 years ago was incredible.

The exhilarating sensation of finding and then grasping an object connected to ancient Saxon warriors brought a reality to their existence that only reading about them could not. I was hooked. Subsequently, I also found a few worn Roman coins in the field and a scattering of further historical items. None of these objects were particularly valuable, but each physical connection to long-forgotten people meant the world to me.

These fascinating finds then inspired me to begin doing some solid research on this lone field at the foot of Lewes and to attempt to find out more about where these items may have come from. With the discovery of every subsequent piece of information on this subject, I started to build an incredible picture of the people who had once roamed this land.

Trying hard to learn as much as I could about these Anglo-Scandinavian folks from the past, I began searching for anything that could help me to get to know them better; this is when I first stumbled across the *Beowulf Manuscript*. Thankfully, the whole story had already been turned into an audiobook, translated and orated by Seamus Heaney, and was available on the YouTube website. Over the following months, I listened to it repeatedly at any opportunity I could get, and subsequently, among the incredibly complicated details, strange names, and old expressions, it dawned on me that there were some very curious parallels in the *Beowulf* story that seemed to loosely match up with the landscape and the research I had been carrying out on the Anglo-Saxon presence near Lewes. At this point, I had also cautiously linked these finds to an ancient church called Old St Peters, situated directly across the river Ouse on the Hamsey promontory. From the information I had learned, it appeared that King Aethelstan had held a "witan" (a meeting of his Ealdormen, much like an early parliament) there in the year 925 AD.

Incredibly curious now and with a specific question in mind, I tasked myself to do some further research. With little hope or expectation, I decided to see if there could be any documented Kings of *England* that might somehow fit into the *Beowulf* story. Immediately, I struck upon something so unlikely that I could not shake the feeling that I had stumbled across a truly improbable but, it would now seem, astonishingly real possibility.

Could *Beowulf* be a factual story? Could he have lived in England and not Sweden? Was it possible that he had been recorded as an Anglo-Saxon King named Beornwulf, who, at first glance, had died in the year 825? Despite the obvious similarity in the names, it appeared that Beowulf and Beornwulf were also both succeeded by a man named Wiglaf. This struck me as a rare name and an unlikely coincidence, given that they were also from the same Anglo-Saxon period of history.

From what I had learned so far, however, Beowulf was supposed to have lived in Sweden and had apparently battled a dragon, so it seemed extremely unlikely that this could possibly be true. Nevertheless, with so many strange connections to the tale, I decided to undertake some in-depth research on this little-known king, Beornwulf, and found that there was scant information available about the man. Still, thankfully, there was just enough to begin to see some highly probable links to the *Beowulf* story. Just enough to keep me searching through historical records for any further connections that I could find.

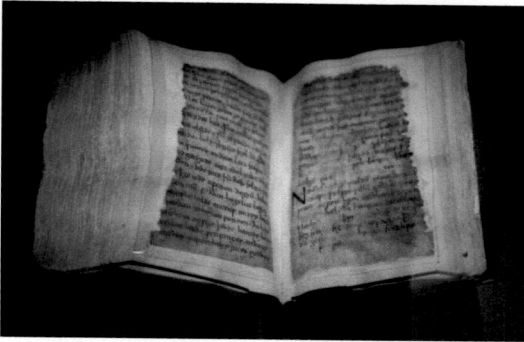

~ CHAPTER 3 ~

ÇEATLAND

For us to understand the highly probable reality of the *Beowulf* story and how it relates to Sussex, Lewes, Hamsey (Hammes), and our known history, it is necessary to examine some critical details within the text.

We should begin by clarifying some vital information regarding the location of Beowulf's home, Geatland. A false assumption has been made here, and this assumption is that Geatland has been definitively attributed to Gotaland in Sweden. This apparent mistranslation has been reiterated so many times that it has actually become the basis for the story's description. In truth, however, there is absolutely no mention of Beowulf being in Swedish lands while at home in Geatland throughout the entire text, although, from the complicated language that is presented to us, it is perhaps understandable why researchers have placed it there.

Within the manuscript, in one of the only mentions concerning the possible location of Geatland in relation to Sweden, a messenger takes the news to the clifftop after Beowulf's death *in Geatland* and declares that he is *from* the Swedish realm; he does not state that they are *in* the Swedish realm. Within these specific lines of the text, we find that this man is declaring that, even though he is from Sweden, he fears that the Swedes will come to fight them now that their great protector, Beowulf, is dead. This implies that despite being a Swede, this man is happily in Geatish lands under the rule of Beowulf, which also suggests that a complicated connection exists between the two tribes.

As previously mentioned, the common consensus among critics and researchers today is that Geatland refers to Gotaland, which is in the southern half of Sweden. They propose that this was a separate country from Sweden in the time of Beowulf. However, we can be fairly certain from examining the text in detail, and taking it at its word, that this supposition is unlikely to be correct.

"Soon was deed of hate and strife <u>betwixt Swede and Geat</u> and <u>feud on either hand,</u> <u>across the water wide,</u> bitter enmity in war, since Hrethel was dead, or else the sons of Ongentheow were bold in war, eager to advance, and desired <u>not to keep the peace across the sea,</u> but about Hreosnabeorg they oft times wrought cruel slaughter."

The Beowulf Manuscript
JRR Tolkien Translation
Line 2076

This is a critical paragraph, for we know that there is no sea in the middle of Sweden that separates the south from the north, and it seems we are being told here that the journey between the Swedes and the Geats *requires* them to cross the ocean. If this is indeed the case, we can completely rule out Sweden or the south of Sweden as the location for Geatland.

We *could* attempt to imply here that the author is writing his story in England and is referring to the Geats *and* the Swedes who are *both* "across the water wide". However, a further detail that we are provided with from the *Beowulf Manuscript* states that the journey between Geatland and the Danish home of Hrothgar takes two days of travel by boat, which would not make any sense at all if Geatland was in the south of Sweden.

"Away she went over wavy ocean, boat like a bird, breaking seas, wind-whetted, white throated, till the curved prow had ploughed so far – <u>the sun standing right on the second day</u> – that they might see land loom on the skyline, then the shimmer of cliffs, sheer fells behind, reaching capes."

The Beowulf Manuscript
Michael Alexander Translation
Lines 216 – 223

"Driven by the wind, the foamy necked ship then passed over the sea-waves most like a bird, until after the lapse of a normal space of time, <u>on the following day</u> the ring-prowed craft had reached the point where the travellers saw land, ocean cliffs standing out, steep headlands, broad sea-scarps; then the journey had concluded at the far end of the voyage."

The Beowulf Manuscript
RD Fulk Translation
Lines 216 – 224

These lines describe Beowulf's journey from Geatland to Danish Lands on his trip to aid Hrothgar with the problem of Grendel. The Oresund is the name for the body of water that separates Sweden and Denmark. Notably, the journey across this ocean would take just *hours* and not days to complete; so, for the present moment, as I attempt to lead us to an alternative home for

Beowulf using these important descriptions from the text, let us now begin to acknowledge that Geatland may have been in the south of Britain as a completely valid possibility. Astonishingly, given the current consensus, there is absolutely no evidence in the text to suggest otherwise. I can confidently assure you that amongst all of the complicated details, no reference in the entire story confirms Geatland to be in the south of Sweden.

A further detail regarding Geatland is an important gift that Hygelac, Beowulf's lord gives to Beowulf.

After Beowulf sails back across the ocean, returning home from his successful mission, he presents Hygelac with the treasures he has been gifted by Hrothgar at the great hall of Heorot, somewhere over in Danish lands. In return, Hygelac gives Beowulf many great rewards, including kingship and 7000 hides of land in Geatland.

> *"The battle-famed king, bulwark of his earls, ordered a gold-chased heirloom of Hrethel's to be brought in; it was the best example of a gem-studded sword in the Geat treasury. This he laid on Beowulf's lap and then rewarded him with land as well, <u>seven thousand hides</u>, and a hall and a <u>throne</u>. <u>Both owned land by birth</u> <u>in that country</u>, <u>ancestral grounds</u>; but the greater right and sway were inherited by the higher born."*

> *The Beowulf Manuscript*
> *Seamus Heaney Translation*
> *Line 2,190*

Here, we have been provided with an exact figure and a measurement description of "hides" for the land that Hygelac gifts to Beowulf. We have also been informed that these are ancestral lands.

At this point, it is important to know that the name Sussex originates from the Old High German "Suthseax" (South

Saxon). This is noteworthy because the first Saxon invaders to arrive and settle in England are recorded as landing in Sussex.

Anglo-Saxon Chronicle ~ Year 477

477. In this year, Aelle came to Britain and his three sons Cymen, Wlencing, and Cissa with three ships at a place which is called Cymensora, and there slew many Welsh and drove some to flight into the wood which is called Andredesleag (Sussex Weald).

The next notable clue is that the recorded size of Sussex (ancestral lands) is preserved for us in an early document with precisely the same measurement of "seven thousand <u>hides</u>"

1	*Myrcna continet*	30000	**Hidas.**
2	*Wocen-setna*	7000	hid.
3	*Westerna*	7000	hid.
4	*Pec-setna*	1200	hid.
5	*Elmed-setna*	600	hid.
6	*Lindes-farona*	7000	hid.
7	*Suth-Gyrwa*	600	hid.
8	*North-Girwa*	600	hid.
9	*East-Wixna*	300	hid.
10	*West-Wixna*	600	hid.
11	*Spalda*	600	hid.
12	*Wigesta*	900	hid.
13	*Herefinna*	1200	hid.
14	*Sweordora*	300	hid.
15	*Eyfla*	300	hid.
16	*Wicca*	300	hid.
17	*Wight-gera*	600	hid.
18	*Nox gaga*	5000	hid.
19	*Oht gaga*	2000	hid.
20	*Hwynca*	7000	hid.
21	*Ciltern-setna*	4000	hid.
22	*Hendrica*	3000	hid.
23	*Unecung-ga*	1200	hid.
24	*Aroseatna*	600	hid.
25	*Fearfinga*	300	hid.
26	*Belmiga*	600	hid.
27	*Witherigga*	600	hid.
28	*East-willa*	600	hid.
29	*West-willa*	600	hid.
30	*East-Engle*	30000	hid.
31	*East-sexena*	7000	hid.
32	*Cant-warena*	15000	hid.
33	*Suth-sexena*	7000	hid.
34	*West-sexena*	100000	hid.

Henry Spelman's *Glossarium Archaiologicum*, published in 1635 as is found in precisely the same format within the *Beowulf Manuscript*. Thankfully, we are fortunate to have a surviving original copy of *The Tribal Hidage*, from an edition of Henry Spelman's *Glossarium Archaiologicum* to confirm this:

Please note number 33, Suth-Sexena 7000 hid – "South Saxons – 7000 hides"

To further support the possibility that Geatland was in the South of England, there is another important clue for us to find in the historically recorded name, Scylding.

Scylding
Wikipedia

According to legends, the Scyldings (OE Scyldingas) or Skjǫldungs (ON Skjǫldungar), both meaning "descendants of Scyld/Skjǫldr," were a clan or dynasty of Danish kings that conquered and ruled Denmark, Sweden, <u>part of England</u>, Ireland, and North Germany.

Hrothgar, the Danish King who Beowulf sails across the ocean to assist with the problem of Grendel, is recorded as being a Scyld. He also has many other titles that we will cover in a later chapter. The first key point to note here is that Hrothgar is the ruler of *many* nations, as is confirmed in the geography of the Scylding reference above. The second point is that Beowulf himself is linked to this family by his own ancestry and that the Scyld name may also be tied to the introductory scene in the *Beowulf* text. This early part of the tale deals with the funeral of a man called Shield Sceafing, who we can connect to the following legend regarding the origins of the Scyldings.

Sceaf
Wikipedia Reference
Descent from Sceaf
Sceaf § Variations on Sceaf's lineage

According to Anglo-Saxon legends recounted in Widsith and other sources such as Æthelweard (Chronicon), the earliest ancestor of Scyld was a culture hero named Sceaf, who was washed ashore as a child in an empty boat, bearing a sheaf of corn. This is said to have occurred on an island named Scani or Scandza (Scania), and according to William of Malmesbury (Gesta regum Anglorum), he was later chosen as King of the Angles, reigning from Schleswig. His descendants became known as Scefings, or more usually Scyldings (after Sceldwea). Snorri Sturluson adopted this tradition in his Prologue to the Prose Edda, giving Old Norse forms for some of the names.

"Famed was Beowulf, far spread the glory
Of Scyld's great son in the lands of the Danemen."

The Beowulf Manuscript
Lesslie Hall translation

This reference is in relation to an early ancestor of Beowulf who is also called Beowulf.

All of this information will become far more relevant as we proceed, but to continue, let us now learn of the historical King Beornwulf of Mercia and the interesting information we have available that helps us to link him to Beowulf.

~ CHAPTER 4 ~

BEOWULF AND BEORNWULF

To begin this chapter, it would be useful to make a brief yet informative etymological examination of the names Beowulf and Beornwulf. Incredibly, there is a highly probable link to Roman Gladiators to be found here, which may explain the otherwise curious irrelevance of the title "Beow" wulf.

The Old English word "beow" translates directly to the Modern English "barley". This seems somewhat strange in relation to the heroic character of Beowulf. However, it has recently come to my attention that Roman Gladiators were once known as "Barleymen". The reason for this curious title is that Gladiators were known to eat substantial amounts of barley during their fighting years. The barley, in turn, provided them with cheap, carbohydrate and protein-rich food, essential for high energy output, building muscle, and maintaining a small layer of fat. This is precisely what a Gladiator or any active warrior would require to function well.

With this newly discovered connection, it seems probable that there is a crossover between the "Barleymen" name given to gladiators from the Roman era and the Beowulf name itself, which was possibly a nickname for the gigantic warrior.

It is also interesting to note in relation to this connection, that the beginning of the *Beowulf Manuscript* speaks of an ancestor of Beowulf, who is also called Beowulf. To avoid the obvious confusion between the two characters, the first Beowulf within the text has been shortened to Beow by many of the countless translators, but the original text states, "Beowulf", for this ancestor from an unspecified era. We are also informed that this original, early Beowulf is, for an unspecified reason, incredibly famous. This, in turn, creates a possible link to the period surrounding the Roman departure of Britain, Roman Gladiators, and the (important to this investigation) subsequent settlement of Sussex by Aelle in the late 400s.

The Anglo-Saxon King, Beornwulf, has a very different etymological translation for his name. Beorn translates to "bear" (a cub in the yard). It has also been proposed that Beorn derives from "bearn" (child, offspring, boy, servant). This term is still used today in Scotland in the form of "bairn". We could imply here, then, that Beorn-Wulf is the "son" of a Wulf.

So now let us look at the wulf part of their names. It is fairly obvious that "wulf" translates directly to "wolf". In the modern day, most of us consider the "wolf" name (wolfish behaviour) to be in relation to a sexually aggressive male, but this does not appear to be a correct hypothesis here as we are repeatedly informed throughout the text that Beowulf is decent, true, and not an aggressive womaniser. It has been noted, however, that up to the 12th century, the term "wulf" was used in relation to sexually aggressive females. This early translation comes from the Roman slang for whore or "she-wolf". It seems probable that this second part of Beowulf's name may be in relation to his mother, who we are not given any details of throughout the entire *Beowulf* text. Historically, we also have no surviving information regarding the mother of Beornwulf.

So here we have a small initial connection between the two men, Beowulf and Beornwulf, in the Wulf part of their name and their unknown maternal ancestry. Etymologically, we also now know that Beowulf and Beornwulf translate to Barley Wulf and Bear Wulf respectively, two names that we now know are descriptively, somewhat similar.

Let us now have a look at some further details on King Beornwulf, who is poorly represented in the *Anglo-Saxon Chronicle*. In the only entry in which he is mentioned, Beornwulf is almost a side note.

Anglo-Saxon Chronicle
Year 823 (825)

825: In this year there was a battle at Galford between the Britons of Cornwall and the men of Devon. And the same year, King Egbert and King <u>Beornwulf</u> fought at Ellendun, and Egbert was victorious and great slaughter was made there. Then he sent his son Aethelwulf from his levies and Ealhstan, his bishop, and Wulfheard, his ealdorman, to Kent with a great force, and they drove King Baldred north over the Thames, and the Kentishmen submitted to him and the men of Surrey and Sussex and Essex, because formerly they had been forced away from {their allegiance to} his kinsmen. And the same year the king of the East Angles and his court turned to King Egbert as their protector and guardian against the fear of Mercian aggression; and the same year the East Angles slew Beornwulf, king of the Mercians.

Further details we have available on Beornwulf, extracted from articles based on charter evidence and the Anglo-Saxon Chronicle

Beornwulf Rex.
King, 823-826.
Died in the year 826.

Present at the Clovesho Witans (from charter evidence) from 812 to 826.

Low position in charters early on, yet subsequently became king.

The current consensus is that he was defeated (but not killed) at the battle of Ellendun, fighting against King Ecgberht and Prince Aethelwulf in 825. He died one year later.

He was supposedly succeeded by Ludecan (possibly a brother of Beornwulf). The historical King Wiglaf took the throne in the year 827.

Footnote regarding Beornwulf.
Anglo-Saxon England by F.M. Stenton pg 229

A man named Beornwulf is mentioned as having witnessed a charter of King Coenwulf in 812 and another of King Ceolwulf in 823, but his position on each of these charters suggests that he was not of an exceptionally high rank. Beornwulf deposed Ceolwulf I in 823.

As we can see here, King Beornwulf is preceded by King Ceolwulf 821-823 and King Cenwulf 796-821. This detail is immediately noteworthy, as it gives us a solid link to the beginnings of Anglo-Saxon literature, of which *Beowulf* is a part. This literature comes in the form of a publication that is still available today: *The Old English Poems of Cynewulf*. King Cynewulf 757-786 ruled Wessex prior to Cenwulf and Ceolwulf. This beautiful and equally rare early Anglo-Saxon text concentrates on the great theme of the time, Christianity. Of these incredibly scarce Anglo-Saxon texts we have available to us then, it is crucial to recognise that Cynewulf was king only 37 years prior to Beornwulf and that *The Old English Poems of Cynewulf* may have been composed near to the time of the great epic *Beowulf*.

Let us now examine two rare coins attributed to King Beornwulf, below.

A silver coin of Beornwulf

This picture has now been changed on the Wikipedia page

Please take note that the specific coin above, once presented to us on the Wikipedia page for Beornwulf, reads "BeorHwulf". (The *P-like* letter after the *H* is the Anglo-Saxon letter wynn, which later became our letter, W). We can confirm that this is indeed an H and not an N, as other coins of Beornwulf have survived, which clearly show an N (below). It is also noteworthy to recognise that the name on the coin above reads "Beorhwulf", which sounds identical to

"Beowulf" when spoken aloud, and that this coin, for some reason, has been assigned to Beornwulf.

Further coin of Beornwulf, which clearly displays an N – BeorNwulf Rex.

This specific coin, one of only 25 in existence, was found "near Lewes"

So, let us now see if we can find any further connections between the manuscript character, Beowulf, and the historical character, Beornwulf, from the little information we have available.

"Long was he contemned, for the sons of the Geats did not account him worthy, nor would the king of the windloving folk accord him a place of much honour upon the seats where men drank mead. They much misdoubted that he was of sluggish mood, without eager spirit though of noble birth. A change and end of all his heart's griefs had come for him, a man now blessed with glory."

(Description of Beowulf)
The Beowulf Manuscript
JRR Tolkien translation
Line 1830

As we can see from Tolkien's translation of *Beowulf* and Stenton's reference to Beornwulf as being "one of the less distinguished ealdormen of the Mercian kingdom", both men are deemed "low in esteem/rank" early in their lives, yet both men also rise to become kings. If we now consider the remarkable similarity in these kings' names and then we include the Wiglaf characters that succeed Beornwulf in our historical records and Beowulf in the manuscript, we can start to see an unlikely but factual link between the two. There is only one King Wiglaf in history, and he is recorded as the king who took the throne just one year after the death of the historical King Beornwulf. In the *Beowulf* text, Beowulf leaves his Kingdom to Wiglaf. So, except for two letters in a name and less than one year between the two Wiglaf characters' reigns, we come remarkably close to an identical link with the *Beowulf* story that occurs nowhere else in recorded history.

"You are the last of us, the only one left of the Waegmundings. Fate swept us away, sent my whole brave, highborn clan to their final doom. Now I must follow them."

That was the warrior's last word.

(Beowulf speaks his final words to Wiglaf)
The Beowulf Manuscript
Seamus Heaney Translation

Anglo-Saxon Chronicle
Beornwulf, Ludeca and Wiglaf

823. In this year, Ceolwulf was deprived of his Kingdom.

824. In this year, two ealdorman, Burnhelm and Muca, were slain, and there was a synod (witan) at Clofeshoh

825. In this year there was a battle at Galford between the Britons of Cornwall and the men of Devon. And the same year, King Egbert and King Beornwulf fought at Ellendun, and Egbert was victorious and great slaughter was made there.

827. In this year, Ludeca, king of Mercia, was slain and his five ealdorman with him, and Wiglaf succeeded to the Kingdom.

───────────────────────────

An important point to acknowledge here is that the *Anglo-Saxon Chronicle* entry for the year 825 states that Beornwulf was slain in that same year by the East Angles. If Beornwulf was truly Beowulf, this detail does not match the *Beowulf Manuscript* regarding his death. It is noteworthy, however, that this is either an error or a later addition to the end of this entry and that it is incorrect. Beornwulf did not die in the year 825, as is stated here. We can be confident of this, as he is recorded as a witness to a recorded charter written in late November 826 (below). This may be a scribe's error based on the information he had available at the time, or perhaps this is a later addition to the *Anglo-Saxon Chronicle* entry of 825, inserted as a subversion to the truth. We may never know, but the possibility of overlap between the characters Beowulf and Beornwulf remains open. It is also notable that using this alternative date for the death of Beornwulf, there is now *no* gap between the reigns of the historical King Beornwulf and King Wiglaf, *precisely* as we find within the *Beowulf Manuscript*.

───────────────────────────

Beornwulf
Wikipedia

Beornwulf rebuilt the Abbey of St. Peter, and he presided over two synods at Clofesho (an unknown location believed to be near London) with Archbishop Wulfred of Canterbury in 824 and 825. A Kentish charter shows that Beornwulf still had authority in Kent on **27 March 826** – S1267, issued on that date, is said to be in the third year of Beornwulf's reign. Coins minted during Beornwulf's reign are very rare, with only around 25 known examples.

It is also noteworthy, for future reference, to examine the critical wording and subsequent interpretation of the following line from the *Anglo-Saxon Chronicle* entry for 825:

Anglo-Saxon Chronicle

Year 825 – And the same year, King Egbert and King Beornwulf fought at Ellendun, and Egbert (Ecgberht) was victorious and great slaughter was made there.

From the currently accepted interpretation of this sentence, we are given the impression that Ecgberht and Beornwulf are fighting *against* each other here, and, at first glance, that seems to be the case, but in reality, this purely depends on the readers' interpretation. We could equally imply that Ecgberht and Beornwulf fought *together* at Ellendun, and Ecgberht (as the king the scribe favoured) was victorious against Baldred, who, in the next line, is described as being driven out of Sussex and Kent and across the Thames. Either scenario is possible based on the choice of words the scribe has used. We cannot know definitively, but both possibilities should remain open to us as we must also note that when describing battles prior to this entry in the *Anglo-Saxon Chronicle*, "against" is used in place of "with".

Anglo-Saxon Chronicle

Year 743 – In this year, Aethelbald and Cuthred fought *against* the Welsh.

Year 750 – In this year, King Cuthred fought *against* Aethelhun, the presumptuous ealdorman.

Year 752 – In this year, in the twelfth year of his reign, Cuthred fought *against* Aethelbald at Beorgfeord.

To remain in keeping, the entry for the year 825 should read: "And the same year, King Egbert fought *against* King Beornwulf at Ellendun". As we can see, it does not say this, which may suggest an intentional subversion of the truth in this record regarding the events at Ellendun. Alternatively, it could simply be a later addition from a new scribe who chose to use different language, but it is vital that we examine all possibilities along the way, as each point may become far more relevant as we proceed. The final two sentences of this specific entry in the *Anglo-Saxon Chronicle* also seem poorly executed and out of place in the quick repetition of "and the same year". The last sentence in the entry, therefore, could have been added at a later date, perhaps to disguise an unwelcome truth.

Of the few historians from previous generations that have commented on Beornwulf, most appear to have labelled him as a highly Christian, pious man, but I cannot locate where the confidence in this idea stems from. It seems to be true that Beornwulf was responsible for building the Abbey of St Peter, a significant name and place that we will discuss further. However, if Beornwulf is indeed the real-life Beowulf, then the construction of this Abbey would not be overly remarkable as Beornwulf lived in a period when Christianity had taken a strong hold in Britain. The early 800s is the perfect time to find Pagan Saxons (Beowulf) converting to Christianity (Beornwulf), just as the language of the *Beowulf* text reflects. To label Beornwulf as *overly* Christian with confidence seems to be an unnecessary embellishment of the truth when the only surviving references concerning his life are a few paragraphs preserved in original documents. I bring this point up, as this assertion may be one of the reasons that no one has connected these two characters in the past.

This point regarding his choice of faith matters a great deal, as it creates a distinct separation between the characters Beowulf and Beornwulf, when there may be none at all. Despite the idea that many of us may have of believing Beowulf and his story to be somewhat Pagan, the *Beowulf* text, when read in detail, is heavily associated with what many scholars have described as a "Christian bias". Could that perceived bias, however, have come about precisely because the story's events occurred during this exact crossover period? I am now confident that this is so, but in any case, it is important to note that there is not enough evidence to suggest that Beornwulf was an overly pious Christian or, equally, that the Beowulf of the story was overly Pagan. The *Beowulf* text implies that Beowulf has a Christian/Pagan background. To begin this journey in earnest, it is crucial that we do not overly Christianise Beornwulf or overly Paganise Beowulf in our imaginations. From the information we have available, we simply do not know. We can only examine the original documents that remain, and it is noteworthy in reference to this that, despite what many people imagine when thinking of the Beowulf story, there is almost no mention of the Pagan Gods in the *Beowulf* text.

The misrepresented idea of Beornwulf being highly Christian provides us with an excellent example of one man's opinion, which has subsequently stuck fast in the minds of later historians. Over the decades, an initial bias in translation has been repeated so many times that it is soon considered as fact. In many instances concerning historical texts, it appears that assumptions and opinions have trumped the original meaning of a simple yet crucial word in its original state. Either accidentally or not, the inability of many historians to remain faithful to original texts, without adding their own "extras" appears to have led to some noteworthy errors that may have drastically skewed our perception of past events.

In relation to this, the general gist of a quote I overheard some time ago is appropriate here. I cannot find a source, but the sentiment is clear.

"History is not simply a study of the past; it is, more accurately, a study of the <u>records</u> of the past."

I certainly agree with this, and it is critical that we keep to the original and authentic words of those records. If we really wish to know the truth, we must throw away our impressions of what we imagine something to be and look only at the truth of what it actually is. With this in mind, I will attempt to point out the errors I have found and state the facts of my findings with as little bias as possible.

Some immediate examples of these additional historical "extras" come to us in the form of the current historical references we are provided with for the place names: Ham, "in Wiltshire", Cyningeston, (Kingston) "by Thames", Ringmere, "in Northumbria", Ashdown, "in Berkshire", and Heathfield, "in South Yorkshire".

The truth of the matter regarding all of these historically

documented place names is that in the original documents, none of the references above actually state the suffixes framed in quotation marks. Not one of the *original documents* places these locations with the suffixes that are provided to us today. These "extras" have all been guessed at, taken up by other historians, and have now been repeated as fact to the extent that most people today simply have no idea that there is little to *no* evidence to support the commonly agreed site identification. Quite often, there is not even any logical explanation to support the theory. We will cover all of these locations as we proceed.

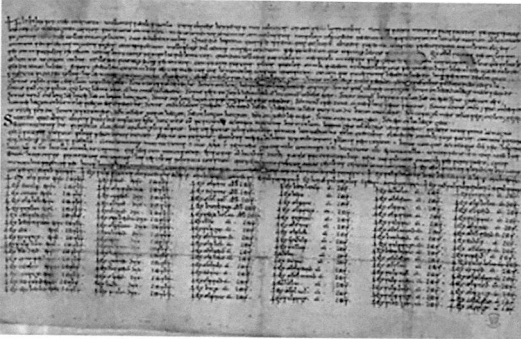

~ CHAPTER 5 ~

THE CHARTERS OF
KING AETHELSTAN

To continue this journey, we must now examine some critical information regarding some of the first parliaments held in British lands. During the early Anglo-Saxon era, these meetings were known as witans. Notably, Beornwulf is recorded in many, and is the ruling king at two of the last recorded councils of Clofesho. The word "witan" is a shortened version of "witenagemot", which translates to "the wise men" (a council of the wise men).

Beornwulf of Mercia
Wikipedia

Beornwulf rebuilt the Abbey of St. Peter, and he presided over two synods (witans) at Clofesho (an unknown location believed to be near London) with Archbishop Wulfred of Canterbury in 824 and 825.

Clofesho
Summary of information concerning Clofesho
Bede's Ecclesiastical History

At the council of Hertford (Herutford) in the year 672, it was decided that, for unknown reasons, meeting at Hertford twice a year would be too difficult. These councils or 'synods' were held to settle whatever matters may have arisen at the time. To remedy this problem, it was unanimously decided that they would meet once a year on 1st August at the place known as 'Clofesho'.

As noted above, the most famous location for these meetings of noblemen was called Clofesho. This important gathering place was used for many centuries by generations of kings. Mysteriously, at some point during the last 1000 years, this site was lost to history, and despite many attempts to pinpoint the location, to date, nobody has succeeded. Thankfully, we have been left with many surviving original charters from these specific witans, as well as additional charters that were created at other locations across the kingdom. These original-source documents describe the matters addressed in each meeting, and it is in one of these witans from the year 930, with King Aethelstan presiding, that we find some tantalising clues to the *Beowulf* mystery.

Before we look at this charter in detail, it would be helpful now to introduce you to a small, isolated, and ancient church in Sussex. This church, named Old St Peter's, sits on a jutting promontory surrounded by a prominent bend in the River Ouse at the foot of Lewes, in East Sussex. Today, this small, isolated landmass is known as Hamsey, yet up to the year

1306, it was known as Hammes. It is important to note here that the field on the opposite side of the river from Old St Peter's church is where I first began metal detecting.

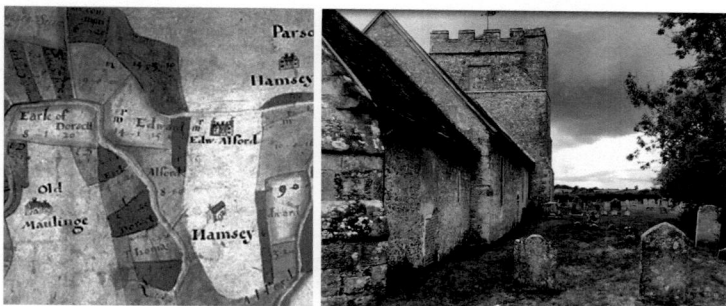

The early name of Hamme or Hammes for this site is a crucial reference in relation to the early Anglo-Saxon period, as this is the only place in England that claims it, as recorded in old charter documents and the *Domesday Book*. We can be certain that it relates to this particular site, as it is linked with Lewes in the earliest recorded versions of its name:

Hamsey

Major Settlement in the Parish of Hamsey

Historical Forms

- **æt Hamme wiþ Læwe** 961 *BCS1064*
- **Hamme juxta Læwes** 961 *BCS1065* 13th
- **Hame** 1086 *DB*
- **Hamme** 1222 *FF*
- **Hamme juxta Lewes** 1309 *FF*
- **Hammes** c.1155 *Lewes* 1439 *IpmR*
- **Hammes Say** 1306 *Ass* 1321 *Ipm*
- **Hammessay** 1342 *Ass*
- **Hammyssay** 1465 *Pens*
- **Hampsey, Hamshay, Haunshay** 1509–11 *LP*
- **Hamsay al. Hammes** 1510 *BM*

Etymology

v. **hamm** . There is a wide bend, of the Ouse here. The pl. form is fairly persistent. The family of *Say* or *de Say* are first mentioned in connexion with the manor in 1222 (FF). *Hamsey* is, as it were, *Ham Say* .

If we reverse engineer the current English word for Home, we find that it originates from "Hammes". The shortened version, Ham, was subsequently used as a suffix for many Saxon kings' burghs. Their legacies live on in Nottingham from "Snotingaham" in Old English (the homestead of Snot's people). Birmingham from the Old English "Beormingahām", or Hailsham, thought to have come from the Saxon "Haegels Ham", meaning the settlement of Haegel.

Hammes by Lewes, however, is a unique name in the Anglo-Saxon landscape. Unconnected to any particular individual of the Saxon era, it is simply Hammes – (Home). It is also important to note that only five other places in Britain today share the shortened version of this name, and one of these is Hames in Wiltshire. This site has been credited as the location of a place mentioned in an important charter of Aethelstan that we will look at momentarily, but, as we will soon come to see, Wiltshire is the wrong location.

Returning to Old St Peters church and the Hamsey promontory, we must now learn of a critical, historically recorded witan that was held there by King Aethelstan (Alfred the Great's grandson) in the year 925.

Friends of Hamsey Website
A Brief History of Hamsey Church

The ancient Church of St Peter, Hamsey, stands on its hillock in a curve of the river Ouse, just north of Lewes. It served as the parish church from *before* the Norman conquest in 1066, and part of the church was certainly standing at the beginning of the second millennium. In 925, King Athelstan had a meeting of his counsellors here, and the Domesday survey of 1086 not only gives details of the manor but adds "there was a Church". In

1321, Sir Geoffrey de Say contracted with John Rangwyn of Offham, mason, to build a large stone hall at the manor of Hamsey; Sir Geoffrey was dead by 3rd March 1322, so if the hall was ever started, it is unlikely that it was ever completed. Some traces of this partial building were still visible in 1777.

Original document referencing the witan of Aethelstan, at Hamme juxta Laewes:

846   SELECT CASES IN

scilicet humiliter bona voluntate dimisit. Insuper pro se et omnibus parentibus suis, natis et nondum natis, nunquam quaerimoniam facturos de praedicta terra, secum acceptis undecim comparibus suis, michi sacramentum fecit. Hoc autem factum est in loco qui nominatur Hamme juxta Laewes. Ego autem Eadgiva habui terram cum libro de Osterlande diebus duorum regum Æthelstani et Eadmundi filiorum meorum; Eadredo quoque rege filio meo de-

ðis aefre gesett sprace waere, and ðis waes gedon on Acðelstanes kyninges gewitnesse and his wytena aet Hamme wið Laewe, and Eadgifu haefde land mid bocum ðara twegra cyninga dagas hire suna. Da Eadred geendude and man Eadgife berypte aelcere are, ða naman Godan twegen suna,

So here we have evidence that King Aethelstan held a witan at Hamsey next to Lewes in the year 925, marking it out as an important location during his reign.

Let us now move on six years from this witan in Hammes to look at a significant paragraph from a charter of King Aethelstan, written in the year 931, in Lifton, Devon. In this charter, Aethelstan is settling a land dispute with an ealdorman named Wulfgar, the name of another character who is also found in the *Beowulf Manuscript*. Here is the relevant paragraph:

Charter of Aethelstan with attached Land Clause
Written in the year 931, Lifton, Devon

"First, go to the east of Ham. Then westward to the mossy bank. Then down to the hedge/boundary of <u>Beow's home</u>, eastward to the blackberry thicket. Then to the black pit/cave. Then north by the head to where the short dyke is. Take out of this one acre, then go to the bird's pond (mere) to the path... After that, to the long meadow. Then to <u>Grendel's lake</u>. Then to the hidden gate, then back east...."

This is an incredibly important reference, as, up to this point in all of our historical sources, no mention of a "Beow" has ever been recorded. I have subsequently found multiple "Beo" prefixes for people that appear to be clustered together in East Sussex and Wessex, but we will cover them in a later chapter on Beorthelmston (Brighton). Even Tolkien, an Anglo-Saxon scholar extraordinaire, was unaware of this "Beow" reference at the time of his translation. This is noted in the extensive afterword to his own translation of the *Beowulf* text by his son, Christopher Tolkien. This critical reference to Beow is unique, and, in addition, in the same paragraph, we also have mention of Grendel, the recorded name of the "monster" from the *Beowulf Manuscript.*

I would now like to provide you with the critical reason for labouring the point on the intricate details of the etymology of Hamsey… In the language used in the original charter, we find that the precise wording is slightly different from the translation provided above. The phrase "Beow's home" is, in fact, recorded as "beowan <u>hammes</u>".

368   ÆDELSTAN TO ABINGDON.   [A.D. 931.

falod peste peardne . þonne norð ofer dunæ on meosh hlinc peste peardne þonne á dune of ða yrfe on beopan hammes hec an on bremeles sceagan easte pearone . þonne on þa blacan grecan. Donne norð be ðam ˈjheafdan to þære scórtan díc . butan án æcre . ðonne to fugel mære to ðam pege . and lang peges to óttæs forda . þanan to pudu mære . Donne to þære rupan hecgan . ðæt on langan hangran . þonne on grendles mære . þonon on dyrnan geat . þonne æft ón linlea geat .

Add. MS. 15,350, f. 82.

Curiously, the original translation of this document, which was undertaken by the only person to thoroughly examine *all* of the preserved charters held within the British Museum, clearly states that this witan was held in Luton rather than in Lifton, Devon (Pg 363 Cartularium Saxonicum, by Walter de Grey Birch). This seems like a curious mistake to make. I am now uncertain which of these locations is correct. No mention is made of this conflicting translation error in any further document that I can find, but I will continue to reference Lifton here as this was a known witan site and seems like a more likely candidate. Perhaps Walter De Grey Birch mistranslated the original spelling for Lifton, which is "Liwtune".

And now, let us look at the words of the second paragraph in the *Beowulf Manuscript*:

> *"To him, therefore, the Lord of life who rules in glory granted honour among men: <u>Beow</u> was renowned – far and wide his glory sprang – the heir of Scyld in Scedeland."*

> *The Beowulf Manuscript*
> *JRR Tolkien Translation*
> *Lines 13-16*

As previously discussed, this is not a reference to Beowulf himself but is found in the opening chapter of the *Beowulf* text, which speaks of the people who came before Beowulf was born. However, we can clearly create a link in lineage from the two names, precisely as the text implies.

So, now let us go on a journey and begin to follow these directions to Beow's home from the land clause above, starting from Old St Peter's Church at Hammes next to Lewes, and see what we can discover.

"First, go to the east" (of Hammes)

This immediately presents a small clue for us. The Ham in Wiltshire that modern historians have guided us to as the location described in the charter, is a reasonably large and unreferenced borough, so the question here should be: Where *precisely* in Ham in Wiltshire would you go eastward from? The Hammes next to Lewes does not present this problem as it is a small area, with a landmass that ends eastwards at the tip of a narrow promontory. Here, we have a precise location to go eastwards from and, in addition, we already have confirmation of a witan that was held there just six years before the date of this charter, presided over by King Aethelstan. There are *no* known witans that took place at Ham in Wiltshire that I can find mention of. Perhaps this is an additional early translation error that has not been addressed until now.

The references provided to us in the description of the land clause appear to support a known place in a specific location. Many of the descriptions are relatively vague, such as: "the blackberry thicket", "the bird's pond", and "the hidden gate". With this in mind, let us now take a look at some useful evidence that we can find across the river from the church, eastwards from Hammes, at the foot of Lewes.

First of all, we have a little-known yet critically important site in relation to this investigation. This large piece of sloping ground is an incredibly rare Pagan-Saxon burial ground that was partly destroyed during the construction of a road at Earwig Corner in 1830. Although initially unknown to me when I first approached the farm owner for access, this is the same land containing the field in which I first began metal detecting.

Mill Road History
Early history: Archaeological finds
Lewes History Group (online)

Excavations in the Malling Hill area have proved it fairly rich in archaeology. In 1830, during the roadworks that altered the course of the main turnpike route between Lewes and Uckfield, a large, <u>high-status</u> Saxon cemetery containing about 20 skeletons was found opposite the first milepost from Lewes at Earwig Corner. Among the objects found were swords, spearheads, knives, shield bosses, iron buckles, two small earthen vessels and a rare bracelet of green glass, either Roman or early Saxon, now exhibited in the British Museum.

An excavation in 1973 uncovered another Saxon burial pit containing the well-preserved remains of 13 young men lying irregularly over one other, face down and in a position that suggested that their hands had been tied behind their backs. Some of them had received fatal blows to the head. A further excavation of the same site in 2005 revealed nine more bodies, from which only one head was recovered. The burials were apparently victims of execution. Carbon dating produced an estimate between 810 and 910 AD.

(This dating works extremely well in conjunction with King Beornwulf of 825.)

So clearly, with the swords found at the site by Earwig Corner, we must have an extremely rare, high-status Pagan-Saxon burial site. In addition, a possibility that appears either wholly unrecognised or is known but undisclosed information regarding this old burial ground, is that it extends all the way up the side of the ancient escarpment it sits beneath, Malling Hill. Here, we can find many mounds of various proportions, now described (but not always) as chalk-pit tailings. I am heavily inclined to disagree with this. Some of these earth formations seem to be large burial mounds, remarkably similar in appearance to those found at Sutton Hoo in Suffolk, the site of two Anglo-Saxon cemeteries dating from the 6th and 7th centuries that included an undisturbed ship burial.

Some of the mounds at Malling Hill may *also* be large enough to hold a ship burial, and I will not be surprised if that discovery is made there someday. Well-conducted archaeological investigations and professional surveys of this site would be interesting to undertake. The finds that I was lucky enough to make in the field below these mounds appear to be items that were churned up in the creation of the road and were subsequently missed during the excavations there.

I am uncertain of what lies deep below the surface of this field, but in all the time I was detecting there, I did not come across any bones to suggest there were still burials present in this particular area. As this field would once have been located right at the *old* shoreline (we will discuss this shortly), perhaps the location of the mounds and burials began precisely where the road now runs. Alternatively, perhaps they were once present in the field but have now been thoroughly destroyed by the plough. It is undoubtedly a site that warrants some attention, but I personally found no evidence of further burials in this field.

Moving on, let us now continue with some further findings on Malling Hill in the next chapter...

~ CHAPTER 6 ~

MALLING HILL AND THE MEALLINGAS

PLACE-NAMES AND EARLY SETTLEMENT IN KENT By P. H. REANEY, LITT.D., PhD, F.S.A.1

It has long been recognised that certain place names are of an ancient type and that their distribution throws light on the earliest areas of settlement. Names ending originally in -ingas, such as Meallingas, now Malling, were originally names of people, "the followers of Mealla", and this came later to be used of the place where they lived.

When I first began researching Malling Hill many years ago, I quickly found an etymological reference for the name of this uniquely isolated island of the Sussex Downs, which attributed it *and* Hamsey to, "Aelle", (M'Aelle Ingas). Curiously, this information is now incredibly difficult to find, but here is one reference that is still available:

477AD Aelle and the South Saxons expansion based on Sussex place names.

VillageNet.co.uk

The Saxons now explore to the east heading up the Ouse valley and settle on the Malling Hill, (Maellingas – Aella's people) where the current South Malling lies. The likelihood is that the legends of a battle near Mount Caburn were probably due to the Saxons defeating the Welsh near Mount Caburn. The Saxons would have been able to sail up the Ouse Valley beyond Lewes as it would have been a tidal estuary at the time.

I have recorded further references, and thankfully, texts on related subject matter still remain. The Mealla that the first reference above relates to is still considered to be the brother of Aelle, which is noteworthy, as we will now come to see in these references from the *Anglo-Saxon Chronicle*, that we looked at briefly earlier on.

Anglo-Saxon Chronicle

477: In this year, Ælle and his three sons, Cymen, Wlencing and Cissa, came to the land of Britain with three ships at the place which is named Cymen's shore, and there killed many Welsh and drove some to flight into the wood called Andredes leag.

485: In this year, Ælle fought against the Welsh near the margin of Mearcred's Burn.

491: In this year, Ælle and Cissa besieged Andredescester and killed all who lived there; there was not even one Briton left there.

The Welsh mentioned here are actually "Weallas" and do not refer specifically to people from Wales. It is an old name for the Celts who also lived in the South of England. "Andreadescester" is thought to be Pevensey, or near Pevensey.

Now, let us look at one of the extremely rare references for Mealla from an article by David Slaughter.

Mealla
www.historyfiles.co.uk
The Northgyth Quest Hypothesis
David Slaughter

Presumed here to have been a royal alderman and Aelle's younger brother. As such, he may also have been the leading warrior in his warlord brother's retinue until Cissa Aelling reached his majority at the age of fourteen. If Mealla was Aelle's brother, he would probably have landed with Aelle near Selsey in 477 and is likely to have campaigned with his brother during the nascent years of Sussex.

In 491, with Aelle having destroyed the Roman fort of Pevensey, it could have been Mealla who defeated the local Britons who were making their last stand on Caburn (Old Welsh 'Caerbryn'). Perhaps it was after this British defeat that Mealla founded his own <u>settlement</u>

not far from the Caburn battle site <u>at South Malling</u>. This theoretical version of events seems to fit the contemporary circumstances.

Once recorded and acknowledged as an Anglo-Saxon settlement site, this area is now described as a chalk pit and has subsequently become an SSRI nature reserve. Current archaeologists make no further mention of this settlement or of the history in this area. It should also be noted that this "Mealla" character seems to have materialised out of thin air. After many hours of searching, there appears to be no reference to this individual in any surviving charter or any reference to him in any book pre-the 1970s. I am at a complete loss as to where this "Mealla" idea has come from. Perhaps I am missing some information, but the available evidence would seem to imply that Malling Hill takes its name directly from Aelle (M'Aelle-ingas). It seems extremely odd that this Mealla character appears to have popped up from nowhere, is connected to Malling Hill, and is additionally "presumed to be" Aelle's brother. I would like to see the original written evidence that implies this, but I cannot find any document to support this theory.

Despite the additional archaeological discovery of many skeletons who are suspected to be executed Viking marauders and who were found in incredibly close proximity to this settlement, no further investigations of this important site appear to have been made. If we also take into consideration the rare, high-status burial ground found at the foot of Malling Hill and opposite Hammes (a uniquely Anglo-Saxon place name), we should perhaps ask why none of this information has been thoroughly investigated. This is possibly a simple oversight or perhaps just a failure to connect the dots, but the distancing of ancient history from this area of England seems to have occurred on multiple occasions.

A notable example is the excavation of an enormous burial mound that sits on top of Malling Down, clearly visible from the top of Lewes High Street. It was excavated in the 1800s by the renowned palaeontologist Gideon Mantell, but nothing was reported on what was found. This burial mound now sits between two fairways of a golf course, silently speaking of the tragically lost archaeology it may have provided us with. More recently, a significant discovery dubbed "the Near Lewes hoard" was made, and barely any mention of it has been made.

This fervent excavation of burial mounds in and around Lewes during Gideon Mantell's lifetime appears to have taken place repeatedly, with no restrictions on this activity whatsoever. We can only guess what was recovered from these burial mounds and was not subsequently recorded. Gideon Mantell's autobiography briefly discusses some of these excavations and additionally, the sale of many of these items to the British Museum. M.G Welch produced two entire volumes detailing further excavations of hundreds of additional Pagan-Saxon and Anglo-Saxon burials in this area of Sussex.

~ CHAPTER 7 ~

THE RING DANES, RINGMER, AND THE BATTLE OF RINGMERE

Continuing our journey eastwards from Hammes, just past Malling Hill and the ancient high-status burial ground, the first settlement we come to just a few hundred yards away is a beautiful old village called Ringmer. Before we begin to examine Ringmer itself and the remarkable host of connections to the *Beowulf* story to be found there, it is critical that we first learn of an important and notably "lost" battle site and the details we have regarding that battle. Various researchers have placed this battle site all over the country, but all of them appear to have ignored one of the only places in existence that claims the recorded name. This battle is referred to as the Battle of Ringmere, which took place in the year 1010. Ringmer in Sussex adjacent to Malling Hill and Hammes, as noted on an old map, *John Speed's Saxon Heptarchy*

1610 (see page 51), was also once known as Ringmere.

The Battle of Ringmere
Wikipedia

The Battle of Ringmere was fought on 5 May 1010. Norse sagas recorded a battle at Hringmaraheiðr; Old English Hringmere-hæð, modern name Ringmere Heath.

In his Víkingarvísur, the poet Sigvat records the victory of Saint Olaf who, according to Norse sources, was fighting together with King Ethelred over Ulfcytel Snillinger:

Yet again, Óláfr caused a sword assembly [BATTLE] to be held for the seventh time in Ulfcytel's land, as I recount the tale. The offspring of Ælla stood over all Ringmere Heath; there was slaying of the army there, where the guardian of <u>Haraldr's inheritance</u> [= Óláfr] caused exertion.

John of Worcester records that the Danes defeated the Saxons. Over a three-month period, the Danes wasted East Anglia, burning Thetford and Cambridge.

It is also noted in the *Anglo-Saxon Chronicle* that (a later) Aethelstan is killed in this battle. The Aethelstan that they are referring to was still an important man, a nephew to the king.

In the reference above, we are told that the people of Aella are standing over all Ringmere heath. We have just discussed the origins of Malling Hill *(Meallingas)*, so in this location, we now have the people of Aella and/or Mealla, located next to a site called Ringmere, with a known, heavy Anglo-Saxon presence. We also have a descendant of the king called Aethelstan in the fight, a high-status burial ground nearby, Hammes, the location of a witan held by the original King Aethelstan in the year 925, and "Harlaldr's inheritance" (Beddingham). These are all self-explanatory links to the location of the battle, and they gain further weight when we subsequently examine three additional battle sites (two of which are also lost). These are called Terrible Down, Heathfield and Ashdown.

If we continue north on the main road past Ringmer village, we first arrive at Terrible Down, a battle site of confused origins. Moving onward from here, along the same road, we then arrive at Heathfield. And lastly, adjacent to Heathfield is Ashdown Forest. So here we have Ringmere, Terrible Down, Heathfield and Ashdown Forest. The three lost battle sites are again: "the battle of Ringmere", "the battle of Heathfield", and "the battle of Ashdown". The similarity between these place names and the battle site names, coupled with the fact that all of these locations can be found on *one* road, is a notable and astounding coincidence. In addition, once we have established many further details on our journey of discovery within this book, we can, with a high degree of probability, assign these lost battle sites to these new locations with a fair degree of confidence.

There is a highly logical reason for placing these battle sites in these locations, and that comes to us in the form of the Andredaeswold (now named the Weald) and the colossal amount of iron ore that was once extracted from the woodland there. Iron was a precious resource during the Roman and Anglo-Saxon eras. Armour, weaponry, tools, rivets, nails, and coinage all required a steady supply of Iron. The Weald is known to have been utilised for this very purpose since the beginning of the Roman invasion. During this time, the Romans processed an estimated 750 *tons* of iron ore from this area *every year*. The discovery of vast numbers of Roman Bloomeries (iron smelting pits) are well documented here, and the primary access to them from the sea would have been found through the tidal sea waters of the Ouse Valley, which once ended at Lewes and Hamsey. Here, it meets with the old Middewinde Rivers and a known, *major* Roman road to London (The London to Lewes Way), marked in black in the centre of the image below. Here, via a smaller track, the road then crosses over Malling Hill and Mount Caburn from the junction by Earwig Corner, where the high-status burial ground was discovered (logistically placed), finally joining with another major Roman road to Seaford, beneath Mt Caburn.

Curiously, despite this significant Roman road from London to Lewes ending directly opposite Hamsey, current archaeologists now imply that the Romans were *not* present in Lewes. The notion of this is, quite frankly, not very well thought out. The ill-informed idea that the Romans would build a main road from the end of a known sea valley all the way to London, but then choose not to build around this location is poorly thought out. Given all the evidence we have, we know that they did build here. Very recently, the archaeologist of an extremely large Roman Villa, which was uncovered at Bridge Farm (right next to Hammes and Ringmer), according to his report, appears to be somewhat confused as to why a settlement of the size they have discovered would be located there. Perhaps he is unaware of the old, recorded sea levels and the documented port that was once situated at Hamsey. We will cover Roman Lewes and the Roman connection to Hamsey very shortly.

Please take note of the sheer size and scope of the old tidal estuary, which is accurately represented for the era on the

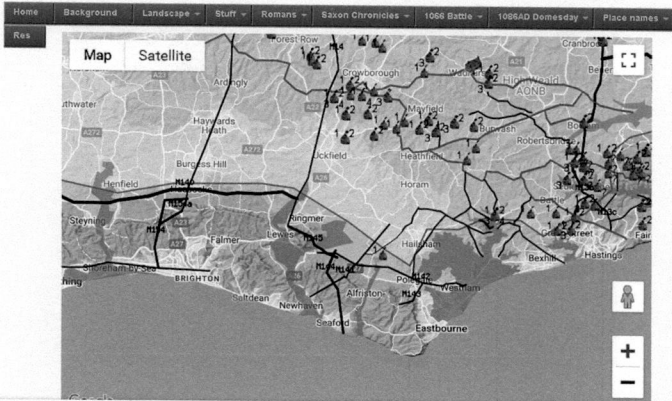

Roman Roads/Bloomeries in the South East centered on Wadhurst Sussex

map above. The prominent situation of Malling Hill, Mount Caburn, Ringmer, Hamsey, and Lewes is incredibly apparent here at this time. It provides us with a fascinating glimpse of a period that may also help us to understand precisely why this sea valley was once so historically important but has largely been ignored in the modern day.

We now need to investigate another of the famous lost battle sites that I previously mentioned. Once again, modern historians have placed this battleground far from East Sussex. The name of this battle is the Battle of Ashdown.

In Ashdown Forest, in East Sussex, which is the known location of the Andreadeswold (frequently referred to in the *Anglo-Saxon Chronicle*), there are two sites with names that may help to give us the precise location for The Battle of Ashdown. The first placename is King's Standing, and the second is Camp Hill. Both of these sites can be found beside the London to Lewes Roman Road, just beyond a junction called Wych Cross. Wych Cross is also located next to a village called Danehill, which I hope needs no translation, and provides us with a further link to the recorded details of this battle.

The Battle of Ashdown
Wikipedia

The Battle of Ashdown was a West Saxon victory over a Danish Viking army on about 8 January 871. The location of Ashdown is not known but may be Kingstanding Hill in Berkshire. Other writers place the battle near Starveall, a short distance north of the village of Aldworth and south east of Lowbury Hill. The West Saxons were led by King Aethelred and his younger brother, the future King Alfred the Great, while the Viking commanders were Bagsecg and Halfdan. The battle is described in the *Anglo-Saxon Chronicle* and Asser's Life of King Alfred.

It is a curious coincidence that the proposed site in Berkshire (referred to above) is called Kingstanding, which is precisely the same name as the hill just beyond Wych Cross in Ashdown Forest called King's Standing. There is no recorded place in Berkshire called Ashdown.

If the information I am presenting is correct, and the Vikings were coming down from the northeast, Camp Hill, being closer to Wessex and Sussex, would likely be the location of Alfred and Aethelred's encampment. Kings Standing would be the staging point of Bagsecg and Halfdan of the Vikings, and Black Hill, in the same location, may denote the location of the battle. With multiple site names that have a possible link to the battle to be found here, it is astonishing that there is no reference for this site being one of the most likely locations for the conflict. However, it is most noteworthy that many strange connections and curious documented incidents can be found within the immediate vicinity of this location.

Harold McMillan, a prime minister of Britain, lived next to Wych Cross in a mansion called Birch Grove. The American President John F. Kennedy visited him there just months before his assassination in Dallas. There are curious allusions to Wych Cross and occultism in a recent T.V. series called *The Sandman*. The notorious occultist Aleister Crowley and his purported son have strong ties to this area and were involved in some bizarre occult rituals there during the First World War. He was cremated in a crematorium on Bear Rd in nearby Brighton. The name Wych is possibly derived from Witch, or the pagan religion, Wicca. The Scientology headquarters in Sussex are also based nearby. Perhaps there is an undisclosed but essential reason that this location has seen such heavy occult-related historical traffic over the centuries. The strangely blatant signpost for a fenced-off Rosicrucian compound located nearby would suggest that this sort of activity is still happening in this area to this very day. Another oddity regarding Wych Cross is that it sits directly on the Prime Meridian.

~ CHAPTER 8 ~

ÇOTE LANE, OLD HAÇ WOODS, HOLT HILL, HAULELAND AND HARLINÇES

ow that we have established some verifiable connections to the Anglo-Saxon presence in this area of Sussex, it would be helpful to re-visit the boundary clause from the charter of Aethelstan, written in Lifton, Devon, to remind us once again of what is written:

"Go eastwards (from Ham/Hammes) to the boundary of Beow's home."

If this is indeed the Beowulf of the *Beowulf Manuscript*, can we now find any further links in the local area to back this proposition up?

The first remarkable connection that links directly to the *Beowulf* text is a road named Gote Lane, which is found just beyond the main route into Ringmer. This road is also located within striking distance of a small, ditched promontory called Middleham, which deserves mention for obvious reasons (the middle of Hammes), and which is connected to the name "Gote" in an old document that we will look at momentarily.

~ Gote Lane ~

Göte means Geat in Swedish. As we have already discovered, Beowulf was a Geat.

Göte
Wiktionary

Göte

Swedish

Etymology

Old Norse Gauti, Gautr ("a Geat", "a resident of Götaland"), from Proto-Germanic *gautaz.

Hygelac began questioning his comrade pleasantly in the high hall; he was curious what the adventures of the Sea-Geats had been: "How did things turn out for you on your trip dear Beowulf, after you suddenly determined to go look for action far over the salt water, combat at Heorot?"

The Beowulf Manuscript
RD Fulk Translation
Line 1,982, pg 217

The oldest map I was able to locate, which includes the name Gote Lane, is held at The Keep, an ancient records archive centre in Brighton. On this 14th-century map, the road name is spelled "Goat". However, in a preserved will left by "Henry, a vicar from Ringmer" in the 13th Century, it is recorded that this road was originally named "Gote". Below is a paragraph from a research paper on the Sexton's Land.

The Deserted Medieval Settlement of Wyke
John Kay

By far the largest of Henry's purchases was the 21 acres of land in the Borgh of <u>Gote and Middleham</u> he bought from Nicholas de Flyngereswyke. This heads the detailed list in his will, where it is described simply as 'At Wick, 21 acres of land'. Its size enables it to be distinguished from many other pieces of Sextons Land in later documents and allows its location to be established.

The next paragraph in this research paper details the connection of this land to Lewes, Glyndebourne, Malling parish, and Ryngmere (Ringmer), but the main focus of this document concerns a lost village called Wick. This ancient settlement was reportedly abandoned during the 14th Century due to a devastating outbreak of the plague. It would seem likely, in relation to this, that the small town that is now located further inland from Lewes, called Newick, may have been created during this same era (New Wick).

~ Old Hag Woods ~

Just beyond Gote Lane, on the narrow road from Ringmer to Glyndebourne, we come to a small woodland with a recorded ancient pathway that leads directly to our next location, Old Hag Woods. To understand the relevance of this name, we should learn how an old hag fits into the *Beowulf* story. Here is the description of Grendel's mother:

Description of *Beowulf*
British Library
https://www.bl.uk/works/beowulf

Beowulf seeks out the hag in her underwater lair and slays her after an almighty struggle. Once more, there is much rejoicing, and Beowulf is rewarded with many gifts. The poem culminates 50 years later, in Beowulf's old age. Now king of the Geats, his own realm is faced with a rampaging dragon, which had been guarding a treasure-hoard.

~ Holt Hill ~

"They hid themselves in Ravensholt, their leader being dead. Ongentheow beset then, with a host outspread, This remnant of the carnage with wounds o'erwearied."

The Beowulf Manuscript
William Ellery Leonard Translation (1923)

If we follow the ancient pathway through Old Hag Woods, just above Glyndebourne Opera House on the outskirts of Ringmer is what was once described as a Saxon hill fort on top of Holt Hill. Although the site is now recorded as a place of no significance, this conspicuous hill fort with a distinctly Saxon name features a rare, triple-ditch defensive perimeter. Now heavily overgrown and tucked away, true appreciation of this location can only be made on the ground.

For the sake of clarity, there is another site in Britain called Ravensholt in the north of England, but as we will see, that area is not linked to the kings of Wessex. Holt Hill by Ringmer, however, adjacent to what now seems to be the location of "Beow's home" and "Grendel's Gatan", can be linked (albeit not definitively) more closely to the *Beowulf* story.

Not in Ringmer itself, but a little further towards The Weald and Ashdown Forest, located near the aforementioned battle sites of Terrible Down and Heathfield, we have:

~ Harlinges ~
(Previously located somewhere between Little Horsted and Framfield)

Harlingen Netherlands
Wikipedia

Harlingen (Dutch: ['ɦɑrlɪŋə (n)] (listen); West Frisian: Harns [hãːs] (listen)) is a municipality and a city in the northern Netherlands, in the province of **Friesland** on the coast of the Wadden Sea. Harlingen is a town with a long history of fishing and shipping that received city rights in 1234.

"The fighters deprived of friends then set out to find their homes, to visit Friesland, residences and tall fortresses. Hengest still remained with Finn, a slaughter-stained winter; he fondly remembered his homeland, though he could not drive a ring-prow on the sea – the deep surged with storms, contended with the wind, winter locked the waves in icy bonds – until another

year arrived among the households, as now still happens, those
which continually observe the time, gloriously bright weathers."

The Beowulf Manuscript
RD Fulk Translation
Line 1,125

~ Halland/Hauleland ~

Just beneath Harlinges on the map above, we can see a small ring fort called Hauleland. This place name translates directly to "Hall Land" and is now named Halland. It is interesting to note that the current spelling of Halland relates specifically to an area in the South of Sweden where Kattegat is located. Kattegat is the proposed location for the home of the legendary Viking, Ragnar Lodbrok, who we will discuss further in a separate chapter. Just beneath Halland is a further reference to Anglo-Saxon history in a little-known (previously mentioned) battle site called "Terrible Down", reference below...

Sussex History Forum
sussexhistoryforum.co.uk

There are two legends about Terrible Down and why it came to be named that way. The first is that Alfred the Great fought the Vikings here and that the slaughter was so terrible that the streams ran red with blood. The second is that Henry III's army, defeated at the Battle of Lewes by Simon de Montford, turned to face their pursuers at Terrible Down and were cut down to a man.

I am far more inclined to believe the first suggestion put forward here as it ties in with King Alfred, who we will soon discover is likely connected to the *Beowulf* story in a genuinely surprising way, and who is definitively connected to the Battle of Ashdown. Furthermore, it would be extremely unlikely that any part of the Battle of Lewes would have somehow made its way over to Halland.

~ Ringmer ~

There is one further critical consideration we should now consider for this area: the name of Ringmer itself. Etymologically, it has been theorised to be connected to "Regni's mere", a Celtic tribe of Sussex during the Roman invasion. However, now that we have established a considerable number of connections to this area in relation to *Beowulf*, could this name be a reference to the Ring Danes of the *Beowulf Manuscript?* An interesting point in relation to JRR Tolkien is that within the *Beowulf* story, the king that doles out golden arm rings to his warriors in the mead hall is referred to as "The Ring Lord", or perhaps, "The Lord of the Rings".

The literal translation of the name Ringmer is "Ring Mere" (Ring Lake/Sea) – This could be in relation to the only isolated "island hill <u>ring</u>" (e.g. Cissbury Ring) of the Downs (Caburn and Malling Hill), which once stood by the sea and was mostly surrounded by the old tidal estuary. This estuary was severely compromised in a great storm that was documented in the year 1287, which completely reshaped the southern coastline of Britain, dumping up to two metres of alluvial river silt into valleys that had previously been accessible by scores of large ships. At this time, I suspect the once thriving Saxon port of Hammes became largely unusable as such, and the critical coastal shipping access to Lewes and South Malling was partially lost. As a relatively rare example of this occurrence, the sea was lost to the land.

The same scenario occurred at Pevensey, where William the Conqueror landed in 1066. When he arrived, he sailed his ships to the foot of the castle. Today, however, the sea is over a mile away. We are told by signposts at the castle that this is due to river silting, but this theory seems somewhat illogical, especially when we examine the sheer amount of land that now sits between these locations and the distant seashore we see today. These old accessible sea valleys were completely reshaped in enormous storms that are barely remembered or remarked on in the modern day. Sea flood silting would be a more accurate reflection of the truth, coupled with higher sea levels recorded during the Roman warm period. Another site that suffered the same fate can be found at Bramber Castle, which I believe is a further critical location. We will cover this subject in detail in a later chapter on the Kings Ecgberht, Aethelwulf, and Alfred.

South of England flood of February 1287
Wikipedia

In February 1287, a storm hit the southern coast of England with such ferocity that whole areas of coastline were redrawn. Silting up and cliff collapses led to towns that had stood by the sea finding themselves landlocked, while others that had been inland found themselves with access to the sea.

The town of Winchelsea on Romney Marsh was destroyed (later rebuilt on the cliff top behind). Nearby Broomhill was also destroyed. The course of the nearby River Rother was diverted away from New Romney, which was almost destroyed and left a mile from the coast, ending its role as a port. The Rother ran instead to sea at Rye, prompting its rise as a port. The storm contributed to the collapse of a cliff at Hastings, taking part of Hastings Castle with it, blocking the harbour, and ending its role as a trade centre, though it continued as a centre for fishing. Whitstable in Kent is also reported to have been hit by the surge.

In all, the storm can be seen to have had a powerful effect on the Cinque Ports, two of which were hit (Hastings and New Romney), along with the supporting "Antient Town" of Winchelsea. Meanwhile, the other Ancient Town of Rye was advantaged.

The storm is one of two huge ones in England in 1287. The other was the one known in the Netherlands as St Lucia's Flood in December the following winter. Together with a surge in January 1286, they seem to have prompted the decline of one of England's then leading ports, Dunwich in Suffolk.

To further support these multiple etymological connections to the *Beowulf Manuscript*, it is useful to take note of the known tradition of assigning the same or similar place names from foreign countries to new settlements in new countries. This can be observed all over the world. A notable and moderately recent example of this can be found in America. Many of the States we find there today are named from the first settlers' English homelands. There are many more examples of this phenomenon. Given the historical evidence, it seems highly probable that the names we have covered here were assigned to these locations to reflect the origins of where the people who lived there first arrived from.

~ CHAPTER 9 ~

BEORTHELM ~ BRICHTHELM BRICHTON, EAST SUSSEX

How Brighton may relate to The Bright Danes, Beowulf, and Hrothgar.

"Now I want to ask you, sovereign of Bright Danes, defence of the Scyldings, one request, that you, protector of fighters, noble friend of nations, not refuse me, now that I have come this far, that I myself, the troop of my men and this company of hardy ones be permitted to purge Heorot".

The Beowulf Manuscript
RD Fulk Translation
Line 426

This paragraph occurs in an early part of the story. Beowulf has departed Geatland, crossed an ocean, and has now arrived where the sovereign of the Bright

Danes resides. He is called Hrothgar. Beowulf has made this sea voyage to attempt to defeat Grendel, an outcast of society who is now wreaking havoc among Hrothgar's people, mercilessly killing his men with a strength he cannot match. The mead hall of Heorot sits empty. In a continuation of this scene, we are given some confusing references we need to briefly examine.

Initially, we are told that Beowulf has gone from Geatland to the land of the "West Danes".

"The blessed Lord in his mercy has sent him to us, to the <u>West Danes</u>, I think, against the terror of Grendel. I shall offer the good one riches for his daring. Be quick about it, direct the band of brothers to appear together in a group; tell them also in a few words that they are welcome to the nation of the Danes".

The Beowulf Manuscript
R.D Fulk Translation
Line 384

On the very next page, however, we have a different reference:

...offered the men of the Geats a word inside: "My victorious lord, leader of the <u>East Danes</u>, has directed me to tell you that he knows your background, and you brave minded ones are welcome to him here over the surging sea".

The Beowulf Manuscript
R.D Fulk Translation
Line 390

So here, the text now calls Hrothgar "leader of the East Danes," but we have just heard him referred to as king of the West Danes.

Strangely, and more in keeping with my thoughts on the

location of Hrothgar, Heorot and Grendel, the revised verse translation by Michael Alexander states on this same line…

"The Master of Battles bids me announce, the Lord of the North Danes, that he knows your ancestry; I am to tell you all, determined venturers over the seas, that you are sure of welcome".

The Beowulf Manuscript
A Verse Translation by Michael Alexander

Perhaps this word was among the lost words on the singed borders of the original copy and was simply guessed at. I am still trying to find the answer to this discrepancy. Prior to both of these references, however, we are given an important clue as to the relationship between these peoples in the many names used for Hrothgar:

Hrothgar made a speech, helm of the Scyldings: "I knew him when he was a child; his father was called Ecgtheo, to whom Hrethel of the Geats gave his only daughter; his hardy heir has now come here to visit a loyal friend. Seafarers who ferried the gifts of the Geats here to our satisfaction used to say that he, brave in war, had the strength of thirty men in his hand grip."

(Hrothgar speaks of Beowulf)
The Beowulf Manuscript
RD Fulk Translation
Line 371

So, what we are presented with here are multiple names for both groups of people: The Bright Danes, The West Danes, The East Danes, The North Danes, The Geats, and The Scyldings. Deciphering precisely who is who is no easy task, but let us try:

Hrothgar is the SOVEREIGN of the Bright Danes.

Hrothgar is the KING of the West Danes.

Hrothgar is the LEADER of the East Danes.

Hrothgar is the HELM of the Scyldings.

Hrothgar is the LORD of the North Danes.

Beowulf is a Geat who are descended from the Scyldings.

The Scyldings are from the line of Scyld, who is a Dane.

Hrothgar is a Scyld.

It would appear from the language used, that Hrothgar is the ruler of many nations: "king of the West Danes", which we are told is in Denmark, "leader of the East Danes", which one would logically assume is not the same place as the home of the West Danes; and "helm of the Scyldings", (protector of). The critical point here is that these are all the titles of people from various places, but the same people, ruled by the same king, Hrothgar and his descendants.

Another essential point to reference, once again, is that they are also crossing the ocean to get from Geatland to the home of Hrothgar in Daneland. As we have now confirmed that southern Sweden could not be the home of the Geats due to the duration and placement of the sea journey, then Geatland would *have* to be located on a different shore "across the ocean" from Denmark, placing the South coast of England firmly on the radar. We also have additional evidence in the *Anglo-Saxon Chronicle* for the settlement in Sussex by Aelle in the year 490, as discussed in Chapter 3.

Let us now look at the definition of a Scylding once again…

Scylding
Wikipedia

The Scyldings (OE Scyldingas) or Skjǫldungs (ON Skjǫldungar), both meaning "descendants of Scyld / Skjǫldr", were, according to legends, a clan or dynasty of Danish kings that in its time conquered and ruled Denmark and Sweden _together with part of England_, Ireland and North Germany.

Now that we have established that these are all different names for the same people and that the Scyldings were documented residents of a "part of England," let us look in detail at the surprising origins of Brighton in East Sussex and see how it, too, may fit into the picture of both Beowulf and Beornwulf.

Brighton Etymology
Wikipedia

The etymology of the name Brighton lies in the Old English Beorhthelmestūn (Beorhthelm's farmstead). This name has evolved through Bristelmestune (1086), Brichtelmeston (1198), Brighthelmeston (1493), Brighthemston (1610) and Brighthelmston (1816). Brighton came into common use in the early 19th century.

As we can see above, the oldest known name for Brighton is "Beorhthelmestun". This translates to the tun (farm) of Beorhthelm (Bright helm), and this name is incredibly relevant. The first reference of this chapter from the *Beowulf* text states, "Now I want to ask you, sovereign of <u>Bright</u>

Danes, defence of the Scyldings..." This Bright Dane reference reverts back to "Beorht Dene". So now we have Beorhthelm, who, thanks to another Anglo-Saxon Charter, we will soon see, is likely a "Beorht Dene" in (or of) "Beorhthelmestun" (Brighton), which is located within a few miles of Beow's home, in Ringmere.

Here, we can also provide a further link to Tolkien, which comes in the form of his recently released work based on the battle of Maldon. Included in this text is the translation of an ancient manuscript. This manuscript is titled *The Homecoming of Beortnoth, Beorthelm's son*. The poem speaks of a battle in East Anglia where Beortnoth, in search of fame, glory and honour, makes a critical mistake in the name of nobility, and subsequently loses the battle and his life. Beortnoth is described as an Earl in the text, so perhaps, as a son of Beorthelm we could imply that Beorthelm (*of Brighton*) was either a King or an important Lord of the era whose son became an earl of East Anglia.

We must now go back to the earlier mention of Clofesho to begin connecting all of this information together, for Clofesho has a stunning, crucial link to the end of the *Beowulf* tale...

~ CHAPTER 10 ~

CLOFESHO/CLOVESHO

urviving to the present day, we have charter records for 300 Anglo-Saxon witans which were held in 116 locations across the country. From the details written within these charters, we know that one of the locations for these witans became far more important than all of the others, and yet today, we do not know precisely where this meeting place was situated. "Clofesho", or "Clovesho", has been described as the most famous lost meeting place of kings in history. Let me remind you once more of the details concerning the founding of this witan site.

Clofesho
Bede's Ecclesiastical History

"At the council of Hertford (Herutford) in the year 672, it was decided that for unknown reasons, meeting at Hertford twice a year would be too difficult. These councils or 'synods' were held to 'settle whatever matters may have arisen.' at the time. To remedy this problem, it was unanimously decided that they would meet once a year on 1st August at the place known as 'Clofesho'."

Subsequent to this date, Clofesho became a significant location, used for many centuries by generations of kings. Mysteriously, at some point during the last 1000 years, it was lost to history. Historians have been searching for this forgotten location ever since.

We should now examine the details of the Charter of Aethelstan, written in Lifton, Devon, in the year 930 once again:

Charter of Aethelstan
Lifton, Devon 930 AD

'First, go to the east of Ham (Hammes). Then westward to the mossy bank. Then down to the hedge/boundary of Beow's home...

Let us now re-visit Old St Peter's Church on the promontory of Hammes. We know with certainty that on, or in the near vicinity of this site, is a location that has been used by King Aethelstan to hold a witan. As there is now only one building from antiquity remaining on this site, which is the ancient church of Old St Peter's, we can assign this historical witan site to the location of this church with a high degree of probability. We also have many etymological connections to the *Beowulf* story in Ringmer and the high-status burial ground on the opposite shore. So, as a hypothetical possibility, let us consider for a moment that Hammes, (specifically Old St Peter's Church) is the true location of Clofesho, and then let us see if we can find anything that might help us to cement this possibility.

Before we lose track of the information we have learned on Beorhthelmestun (Brighton), let us now look at a list containing some of the people recorded at one of the very last Clofesho Witans, held in the year 825, with Beornwulf ruling as King of Mercia.

Clofesho Witan 825 AD
King Beornwulf Presiding
Attendees with a "Beo" prefix to their name:

Beornwulf (King)

<u>Beorhthelm</u> 4

Beorhtsige 9

Beorhthun 5

Beonna 4

Beorhtwulf 1

Beornhelm 3

Beornmod 3

Beornnoth 2

Beornred 2

Here, we have a rather extensive list of Beo's, Beorhts, and Beorn's, with lineages going back up to nine times in the case of Beorhtsige the Ninth. Beorhthelm (Beorhthelmestun/Brighton) the Fourth is also among them.

The proposition that I would like to put forward here is that all of these Beo, Beorn and Beorht characters are of the same people and are, specifically, *originally* from the areas in and around Beorhthelmestun, now called Brighton in East Sussex. Hammes and Old St Peters sit at the foot of Lewes opposite Ringmer; Lewes is a short journey from Brighton via a documented, ancient road. Let us also remember that Beow is recorded as the landowner near Hammes and that Beornwulf is leading the witans at Clofesho in 823 and 825. From all of these connections, we are beginning to build a good case that Hammes and Old St Peters are excellent candidates for the location of Clofesho. Beornwulf is also credited with rebuilding the Abbey of St Peter, and the church on the promontory of Hammes is called Old St Peters (one of many, but a St Peter's, nonetheless). Historians have now placed this abbey, rebuilt by Beornwulf, in Gloucester, but I am aware of no original source document to confirm this supposition.

To further this investigation, let us now examine Clofesho's name itself and see if we can fit that into the geographical scenario we have at Hammes.

Clofesho
Wikipedia

The place name, given by Bede as clofeshoch, is Old English. The first element is clof, a variant of cleófa, 'a cleft, a chasm', while the second is hóh, 'a heel-shaped spur of land'. The modifier, clóf, is a rare word in placenames, Clovelly being the only other certain example of its use in a toponym. On the other hand, hóh is more common, with the densest concentration in the south-east Midlands. This pattern suggests that the place <u>ought to lie within south-eastern Mercia</u>, as has been deduced from the historical evidence.

First of all, we are told here that clof is a "cleft or a chasm". Old St Peter's at Hamsey sits between the peaks of Malling Hill/MtCaburn and Offham Hill, in a narrowing of the valley between the two (in a cleft or a chasm).

Next, we can see that a hoh is described as "a heel-shaped spur of land". Old St Peters Church at Hamsey sits on what can accurately be described as a heel-shaped spur of land, surrounded by the River Ouse.

Both etymological translations already fit very well with our location at Hamsey, but let us now look at a more straightforward translation of this word that appears to have been overlooked entirely, "clofe sho" (a cloven shoe). This is the literal translation of these words. A cloven shoe is a horseshoe. The estuary that once surrounded the hoo (peninsula) at Hamsey is also the exact shape of a horseshoe (this would have been far more obvious when the tidal sea surges reached here prior to the storm of 1287).

Luckily (for my purposes), during the infamous flooding of Lewes in the year 2000, we were offered a brief glimpse of how Hamsey may have once appeared to the Anglo-Saxons and the Romans that came before them. When the river Ouse flooded its banks, it revealed the old coastline and harbour that would once have been present during the life of Beornwulf.

Another critical detail to note here is that Hamsey is described today as a Saxon Island regarding its heritage. This description is a crucial error that we must address. Hamsey *became* an island in 1796 when the Hamsey Cut (Mighell's Cut)

was made. Prior to this date, Hamsey was a peninsula of the mainland, or a "hoo".

The Hamsey Cut
Section of an article on Hamsey
from The Keep website

The church and the site of the original manor house sit on an island formed by a loop in the River Ouse, which accounts for the first element of the placename. The second derives from the name of its medieval lords, the de Say family. As part of the canalisation of the Ouse in the 18th century, <u>the great loop was bypassed by Mighell's Cut of 1796</u>, named after Joseph Mighell, the owner of the manor from 1777 to 1807.

So, to reiterate the point, in Saxon times, Hamsey was a peninsula of the mainland "nigh to the surges of the deep and warring waves"; it was not an island surrounded by a narrow river, as is the situation we find there today.

It is also worth noting that a vast river network once spread far inland, directly from Hamsey. Historically, this river network was called the Middewinde. From the coast to Hamsey, the old tidal sea channel was called the Great River of Lewes. The fresh water from the rivers flowing towards Hamsey meet the tidal sea water from the Southern coast at this precise location beneath the church of Old St Peters to this very day. These fresh and saltwater convergence points are also considered to be significant spiritual locations for many faiths of the past.

The Ouse River (East Sussex)
Wikipedia

'Ouse' is a common name for rivers in England, with examples including the Ouse in Yorkshire, and the Great Ouse and Little Ouse in Norfolk, Suffolk and Cambridgeshire. The name may stem from the Celtic word Ūsa, which is in turn derived from the word *udso-, meaning "water". The root of this word is the Indo-European *wed-, from which the modern English words "wet" and "water" also stem. If this derivation is correct, then its name is a tautology, meaning "Water river" or "Wet river". However, the National Rivers Authority stated that the river above Lewes was called the Middewinde historically, while the river from Lewes to the sea was called "The Great River of Lewes", and that the present name is a contraction of Lewes, with which it rhymes. This claim is also supported by others.

Another name has also been used for the meeting place of Clofesho in surviving literature, and that comes to us in the form of "Cliffe at Hoo". This is also interesting in relation to Lewes and Hamsey. Within a few hundred yards of Hamsey, sailing back along the old tidal channel, we come to Cliffe High Street, which gets its name from the chalk cliffs that it sits beneath, carved out by the lapping of waves that once battered its face. There are very few inland chalk cliffs of such magnitude on the south coast, and there is only one other that can claim the name Cliffe with an "e", and that location has been thoroughly ruled out by other researchers in the past. The Hoo (peninsula) of Hamsey is located just past these cliffs, directly beneath Malling Hill.

Cliffe High Street, with the chalk cliffs in the background

So, whatever way we wish to translate the word: Clofesho, Clovesho, Clofe hoh, Clofe Sho, or even Cliffe at Hoo — they all fit *perfectly* with Hamsey and Old St Peters where we already have evidence of confirmed witans taking place and a high-status burial ground present on the opposite shore.

We also have Beow in Ringmer, Beorhthelmestun nearby, and Beornwulf presiding. This all gives extraordinary weight to the strong likelihood that the true location of Clofesho is Hammes–Hamsey. This will momentarily become even more relevant when we examine some further lines from the *Beowulf* text, and a name for the site that appears to have only been documented once in the charters that are available to us today.

It is now time to move on to some genuinely fascinating observations in relation to the *Beowulf* story that I am sure will leave you as confused, doubtful, and astounded as I was when I first noticed them. In order to comprehend these curious anomalies, and now fully armed with the verifiable history we have learned of in the area so far, we must tackle the complicated details concerning the death of Beowulf and the descriptions of the precise location where he meets his fate.

The death of BEOWULF

CHAPTER 11 ~

THE DEATH OF BEOWULF
AND THE ROMANS

"A newly constructed barrow stood waiting on <u>a wide</u> <u>headland close to the waves</u>, its entryway secured. Into it, the keeper of the hoard had carried all the goods and golden ware worth preserving."

The Beowulf Manuscript
Seamus Heaney Translation
Lines 2,242 – 2,247

"The veteran king sat down on the <u>cliff-top</u>. He wished good luck to the Geats who had shared his hearth and gold. He was

sad at heart, unsettled yet ready, sensing his death. His fate hovered near, unknowable but certain: it would soon claim his coffered soul, part life from limb. Before long the prince's spirit would spin free from his body."

The Beowulf Manuscript
Seamus Heaney Translation
Lines 2,417 – 2,424

"Such was the drift of the dire report that gallant man delivered. He got little wrong in what he predicted. The whole troop rose in tears, then took their way to the uncanny scene under <u>Earnaness.</u>"

The Beowulf Manuscript
Seamus Heaney Translation
Lines 3,028-3,030

Let us begin this chapter by examining the last reference above. In it, we are given a specific name for the site where Beowulf has died: "Earnaness." This translates directly to "Eagle's ness" (Earna = Eagle) and (ness = harbour). So, for an unknown reason, the location where he has died is known as the Eagle's Harbour.

Now let's look at three pictures, the first two taken whilst Lewes was in flood in the year 2000:

1. The promontory or "hoo" of Hammes, where Old St. Peters church sits.

2. The recorded port/harbour that once surrounded it.

3. A broader view of where this old harbour sits in relation to Lewes.

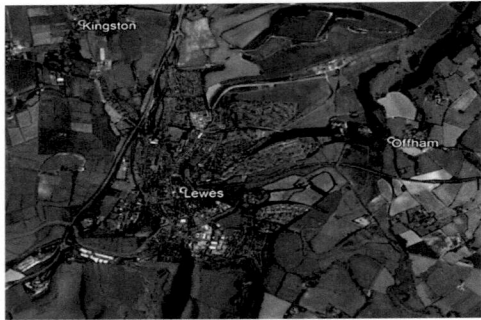

The Tolkien translation gives a slightly different version of this same line:

"Joyless they went with welling tears to the foot of Earnanaes, (Eagles Head) that monstrous sight to see."

The Beowulf Manuscript
JRR Tolkien Translation
Line 3542

This sentence indicates the existence of a harbour found at the foot of "the Eagle". If you have not spotted it already, once we have removed the modern addition of the <u>Landport</u> Estate beneath one of the upswept wings (inexpertly shaded in green) and brought back the old seashore outline during the time of the Romans and the Anglo-Saxons, we are left with this remarkable coincidence…

For this observation to be confirmed as the genuine site of Earnaness from the text, we must now fit all of the other details we are subsequently provided with into the geographical picture we have of Hamsey. This will help us to confirm that what appears to be a bird-like outline of Lewes is not a fluke occurrence and that this is precisely what "Earnaness" is referring to; so, let us now go through them individually:

> ***"Against his will, he went to where he knew a solitary hall of earth, a vault underground, <u>nigh to the surges of the deep and warring waves</u>."***
>
> *The Beowulf Manuscript*
> *JRR Tolkien Translation*
> *Line 2,024*

We have already established that, during the Anglo-Saxon period, Hamsey (Hammes) and Old St Peter's were "nigh to the surges of the deep and warring waves" (see picture above and map on the next page).

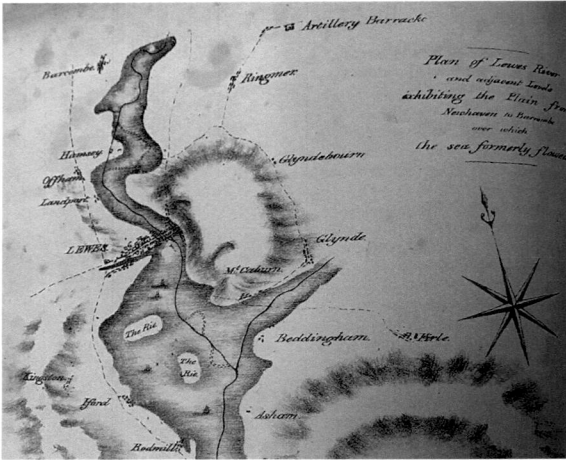

Map of the Ouse Valley, where the sea formerly flowed

The History and Antiquities of Lewes by Rev TW Horsfield and Gideon Mantell

"Now upon the headland sat the war-proven king from whom the Geats had love and gifts of gold."

The Beowulf Manuscript
JRR Tolkien Translation
Line 2,030

We have also established that Hamsey was once a headland and not an island.

"Yet I will not from the barrow's keeper flee one foot's pace, but to us twain hereafter shall it be done <u>at the mound's side,</u> even as fate, the portion of each man, decrees to us."

The Beowulf Manuscript
JRR Tolkien Translation
Line 2,119

This reference could imply that the mound is not just a simple mound but may specifically feature a side. This would make sense when we consider it in reference to the arches that are then mentioned here:

> *"He gazed upon that work of giants, marking how that everlasting vault of earth contained within it those stony arches on their pillars fast upheld."*
>
> The Beowulf Manuscript
> JRR Tolkien Translation
> Line 2,280

This line clearly states that there are large stone arches within this mound, so from this description, we can confirm that it is not a simple burial mound, as modern reproductions of the story have suggested.

In the following reference, we are now provided with a mention of a "vault" within the mound and a further title of note in "the seat".

> *"Then I have heard that speedily the son of Wihstan, when these words were spoken, did hearken to his wounded lord in combat stricken, striding in his netlike mail, his corslet for battle woven, under the <u>barrow's vault</u>. Then, passing by <u>the seat</u>, that young knight, proudhearted, filled with the joy of victory, beheld a host of hoarded jewels, gold glistening that lay upon the ground, marvellous things upon the wall, the very lair of that old serpent in the dim light flying, and ewers standing there, vessels of men of bygone days, reft of those who cared for them, their fair adornment crumbling."*
>
> The Beowulf Manuscript
> JRR Tolkien Translation
> Line 2,309

I do not believe that anyone has ever made sense of what "the seat" could be referring to. It would seem that it has always been considered to simply be the spot where Beowulf is positioned as he lies dying from the dragon's poison. There is, however, a far more logical and accurate translation of this word to be found, which comes in the form of the "seat" of nobility… the lost site of Clofesho, *the* Seat of nobility for the early Anglo-Saxons, and specifically, Beornwulf.

List Of Family Seats of English Nobility Wikipedia

This is an incomplete index of the current and historical principal family seats of English royal, titled and landed gentry families. Some of these seats are no longer occupied by the families with which they are associated, and some are ruinous – e.g. Lowther Castle.

We now need to consider where the arches and stone pillars described in the text may have come from and, more importantly, what happened to them. If we pay sufficient attention to history, it would appear that they must be in relation to the Romans, who are known to have been in these lands just before the Anglo-Saxons and who we also know are the people responsible for bringing the technology of stone arch building to Britain. They are additionally (I believe as a misunderstanding) referred to as "giants" by the Anglo-Saxons in other early documents, just as they are in the *Beowulf* text. To help us identify where this referenced wall may once have stood, we must now look to the old map above, which clearly presents us with an *unnaturally* straight bank to the right of the Hamsey promontory.

As we have already learned, this area was used as a port during the Anglo-Saxon period. I believe that this linear bank was originally a Roman port wall, supported by stone arches that have now been covered with earth, and for a particularly important reason. This concerns an astonishing possibility regarding precisely why this ancient wall may have come to be covered in earth in the first place. It also links into further evidence that explains how a documented treasure hoard of the magnitude described in *Beowulf* may have come to be hidden there. The noteworthy details are found in this entry from the *Anglo-Saxon Chronicle* for the year 418, which concerns the Roman abandonment of Britain:

Anglo-Saxon Chronicle
Year 418

In this year, the Romans collected all the treasures which were in Britain and hid some in the earth so that no one afterwards might find them, and some they took with them into Gaul.

From this significant sentence, we are able to connect this specific *Anglo-Saxon Chronicle* entry directly to the *Beowulf* text. The unusual detail in the sentence is that "some" was hidden in the earth, and "some" they took with them into Gaul. This is a statistically rare example of a divided treasure hoard in literature, and it matches perfectly with the *Beowulf* text when we look at the following paragraph regarding the unknown treasure leavers from generations past:

"There was in that house of earth many of such olden treasures, as someone, I know not who, among men in days of yore had there prudently concealed, jewels of price and mighty heirlooms of a noble race. All of them death had taken in times before, and now he too alone of the proven warriors of his people, who longest walked the earth, watching, grieving for his friends, hoped but for the same fate, that he might only a little space enjoy those long hoarded things. A barrow already waited upon the earth nigh to the watery waves, new-made upon a headland, secured by binding spells. Therein did the keeper lade a portion right worthy to be treasured of the wealth of noble men, of plated gold; and a few words he spake."

The Beowulf Manuscript
JRR Tolkien Translation
Line 1,876

Here, in the *Beowulf* text, we have a remarkable matching detail. The entry from the *Anglo-Saxon chronicle* states that "*some* was hid in the earth". The line from the *Beowulf* text reads, "therein did the keeper lade a *portion* right worthy to be treasured of the wealth of noble men". These are statistically rare examples of divided treasure hoards in literature.

If all of this information is accurate, these accumulated observational details would seem to suggest that Hamsey was once a reasonably large, or well-known Roman port, which then leads us to attempt to identify the possible recorded name of this location during the age of the Romans. In further details found within the *Anglo-Saxon Chronicle*, we have a potential candidate for the port with this reference:

Anglo-Saxon Chronicle

A.D. 449. This year, Marcian and Valentinian assumed the empire and reigned seven winters. In their days, Hengest and Horsa, invited by Wurtgern, king of the Britons to his assistance, landed in Britain in a place that is called *Ipwinesfleet;* first of all to support the Britons, but they afterwards fought against them. The king directed them to fight against the Picts, and they did so; and obtained the victory wheresoever they came. They then sent to the Angles and desired them to send more assistance. They described the worthlessness of the Britons and the richness of the land. They then sent them greater support. Then came the men from three powers of Germany: the Old Saxons, the Angles, and the Jutes. From the Jutes are descended the men of Kent, the Wightwarians (that is, the tribe that now dwelleth in the Isle of Wight), and that kindred in Wessex that men yet call the kindred of the Jutes. From the Old Saxons came the people of Essex and Sussex and Wessex. From Anglia, which has ever since remained waste between the Jutes and the Saxons, came the East Angles, the Middle Angles, the Mercians, and all of those north of the Humber. Their leaders were two brothers, Hengest and Horsa, who were the sons of Wihtgils; Wihtgils was the son of Witta, Witta of Wecta, Wecta of Woden. From this Woden arose all our royal kindred, and that of the Southumbrians also.

Ipwinesfleet is recorded as a lost Roman port that would likely have been located on a limb of the Cinque Ports (five major ports that were used in the defence of the southern coastline). We have already learned that this coastline was reshaped in 1287 by a devastating storm, but we should also now learn of a correlating fact: while the river Ouse *now* runs from Newhaven to Hamsey, in the time of the Romans and the Saxons, the tidal channel was so large, it actually originated in Seaford. Seaford is a known, early Cinque Port. Hamsey, therefore, would once have been on a limb of a Cinque Port. We should also remember that one of the recorded main Roman roads on the far side of Malling Hill made its way directly to Seaford.

Many further Roman sites in this valley are rarely discussed, but the following information can be confirmed with a little bit of digging online. We have a Roman bathhouse at Beddingham and, subsequently, an Anglo-Saxon monastery and church on the same site. There is evidence of a Roman villa with a possible bathhouse next to Hamsey in South Malling (*Archi Maps* online). The recently discovered Bridge Farm Roman Villa is located in this vicinity, just upstream in Barcombe. Ringmer is known to have large quantities of Roman Archaeology. A Roman lead coffin was found at Iford (*Archi Maps* online). During excavations in his back garden, Gideon Mantell discovered Roman Urns in the base of the mound at Lewes Castle. Many other Roman artefacts have been discovered in Lewes; recorded metal detecting finds include coins, fibulas, weapons, and jewellery. Romano British cremation urn burials are dotted all over Malling Hill and Mt Caburn. Mt Caburn, whilst not the highest hill in Sussex, possesses one of the best situations in the whole of the Ouse valley and is known to have been home to a sizeable Roman hill fort.

We looked before at the critical evidence for a significant Roman Road that ends at the foot of Malling Hill by Earwig Corner, directly opposite Hammes. Archaeologists and local historians now appear to be implying that this Roman road (The London to Lewes Way) does not actually reach Malling Hill and Hamsey and alternatively ends at Barcombe. This is incorrect. In M.G. Welch's archaeological record, *Early Anglo-Saxon Sussex*, he clearly states that a burial found beneath Malling Hill is lying directly on the metalling of the Roman road. As per recorded maps, the London to <u>Lewes</u> (not Barcombe) Roman road ended at this precise location – Earwig Corner beneath Malling Hill – because from there, the people of the time would have been able to board a large (for the time) seafaring boat at the port harbour of Hamsey, before travelling on to the coast. As we can see, there is plenty of Roman archaeology here to make this a likely location for the site of the lost port, "Ipwinesfleet".

As a continued observation from my earlier references regarding Roman Lewes, I would briefly like to examine the apparently new, unified stance of modern archaeologists and historians from Sussex who appear to be distancing the Roman presence from the town of Lewes. This was not always the case. In a wonderfully detailed production published in 1824, *The History and Antiquities of Lewes and its Vicinity,* the Rev T.W Horsfield proposes that Lewes was the site of a large Roman fortification named Mutuantonis. Horsfield also makes the case that the streets on top of the hill in Lewes match the known layout of Roman encampments. There are additional unconfirmed rumours of a large Roman villa and bathhouse at a site now occupied by Lewes prison, along with another bathhouse beneath the West Gate car park by the castle. This would make a great deal of sense, but I now

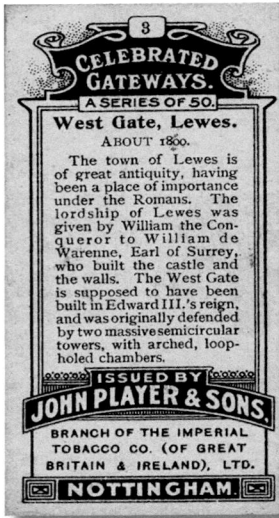

3
CELEBRATED
GATEWAYS.
A SERIES OF 50.
West Gate, Lewes.
ABOUT 1800.
The town of Lewes is of great antiquity, having been a place of importance under the Romans. The lordship of Lewes was given by William the Conqueror to William de Warenne, Earl of Surrey, who built the castle and the walls. The West Gate is supposed to have been built in Edward III.'s reign, and was originally defended by two massive semicircular towers, with arched, loopholed chambers.
ISSUED BY
JOHN PLAYER & SONS
BRANCH OF THE IMPERIAL TOBACCO CO. (OF GREAT BRITAIN & IRELAND), LTD.
NOTTINGHAM.

Old JPS Cigarette Card

wonder if this is in reference to the site of the Pells Swimming Pool in the immediate vicinity. There is a further rumoured site beneath the East Gate chapel at the bottom of Albion St, which I can now find no record of, but this also seems like a likely proposition. "Albion", it should be noted, is a Roman name for the country of Britain; "street" is also Roman in origin. Many additional articles confirm the strong likelihood that a Roman fort site was once situated beneath the church of St John's sub-Castro. Other old references also speak of a strong Roman connection to Lewes:

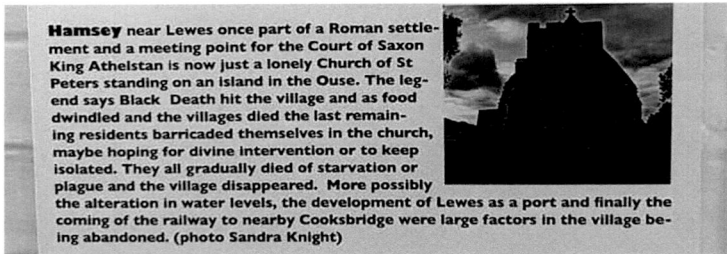

Hamsey near Lewes once part of a Roman settlement and a meeting point for the Court of Saxon King Athelstan is now just a lonely Church of St Peters standing on an island in the Ouse. The legend says Black Death hit the village and as food dwindled and the villages died the last remaining residents barricaded themselves in the church, maybe hoping for divine intervention or to keep isolated. They all gradually died of starvation or plague and the village disappeared. More possibly the alteration in water levels, the development of Lewes as a port and finally the coming of the railway to nearby Cooksbridge were large factors in the village being abandoned. (photo Sandra Knight)

Sign from Pevensey Gaol Museum

Why this information seems to have now been dismissed by Sussex archaeologists puzzles me greatly. The reason I include this information is that ultimately, if we wish to understand how it could be possible for the borders of Lewes to have been set out roughly in the shape of a bird, as I have now presented it to you, the logical answer is that the Romans were responsible. The emblem of Rome was the Aquila (the Eagle), a solid golden effigy of which was carried proudly into battle on the Roman standard. It appears possible that this apparent geoglyph could be a Roman stamp of the Eagle on the earth, created shortly after the early invasions of Britain. We could alternatively attempt to explain this phenomenon away as pareidolia (Pareidolia is the tendency to see faces, animals, or objects in random stimuli), but if this is your immediate conclusion, I would genuinely suggest looking at the outlines of other towns across England and attempting to find another, even moderately bird-like outline of any description. With the use of Google Earth, I have looked at many towns across Britain from a birds-eye view and could not find a single example. With all of the other connections to the *Beowulf* story, Lewes, and its surrounding settlements, Hamsey appears to be *the* Earnaness or "the Eagle's ness" from the *Beowulf Manuscript*. I have no idea how anyone could have accomplished this extraordinary feat, but if any civilisation was capable of achieving this, it would be the highly talented Romans. They certainly managed to build some incredible structures during the height of their power, so I do not doubt for a second that they would also be capable of creating something of this sort.

I have a feeling that the answer to the question of *why* they would create this may be related to the art of subjugation or the phrase, "as above, so below", but it is likely that we will never know the absolute truth of this matter. The Nazca lines are, however, further physical examples of this phenomenon that we can still see today.

Moving on to our next connection, we should now tackle the critical literary detail of the hot spring that flows from beneath the barrow at Earnaness in the *Beowulf Manuscript* to see if we can overcome this additional, gargantuan statistical improbability. Could we actually locate a hot spring at the promontory of Hammes, directly beneath the church of Old St Peter's, where it now seems that the treasure vault of *Beowulf* is located?

> *"Hard by the rock face, that hale veteran, a good man who had gone repeatedly into combat and danger and come through, saw a stone arch and a gushing stream that burst from the barrow, blazing and wafting a deadly heat."*

> *The Beowulf Manuscript*
> *Seamus Heaney Translation*
> *Lines 2,542-2,549*

When I first began researching the possibility of locating a hot spring in this area of Sussex, I feared it would prove to be a probable death blow to my research, a possibility that seemed far too unlikely a detail to present itself in reality. But once again, miraculously, I quickly found the compelling evidence I was looking for.

If we couple this article with the Roman bathhouses in the Ouse Valley, the possibility of locating a hot spring precisely in this location becomes increasingly likely.

For those interested in Arthurian myth, some of these little-known Roman bathhouses of the Ouse Valley may also offer a possible link to the lost "Mt Badon", the

South Downs National Park - Who loves a... ✕

South Downs National Park
Who loves a hot spring? 🌊

While many may know that the South Downs National Park sits on an ancient fault line (giving us natural chalk filtered water for 1.2 million people), many will be unaware of our rare hot springs.

Hot springs in the National Park were first discovered by pre-Roman Belgic tribes who originally used them to brew alcohol before the Romans saw their real value as thermal hot baths.

Over the years the springs have passed between private landowners with no public access.

To mark the South Downs National Park 10th birthday next year, the hot springs will open to the general public for the first time.

With a limited number of tickets available, be quick to grab yours.

🔗 www.southdowns.gov.uk/south-downs-hot-springs-open-2020

site of a battle connected to King Arthur in the original story.

Etymologically, Badon means "bathing hill" from Proto-West Germanic baþōn, the verb being badōn (to bathe).

It is my feeling that the lost Mount Badon <u>may</u> relate to the modern-day Mount Caburn, located on the other side of the disconnected Downland hill ring that includes Malling Hill on the westward slope. We have already discussed the etymology of Malling Hill and the possible connection to Aelle at the Battle of Ringmere. We have also covered the Romano British Hill Fort that was once located on Mt Caburn. Below, we have a further reference to suggest another possible link to this Badon – Caburn hypothesis:

http://biographybase.com/biography/ Aelle_of_Sussex.html

It has been suggested that Aelle led the Anglo-Saxon army at the Battle of Mons Badonicus, possibly as early as 496, though the Annales Cambriae in the Historia Brittonum records the date as 516), and some scholars wonder if Aelle was killed in the battle. This would be a fitting end to the career of the first Bretwalda.

Previously, we learned that the people of Aelle were "spread across the plain" of Ringmere and that Malling Hill is etymologically connected to Aelle or his brother. If we couple this together with the royal/high-status Pagan-Saxon burial ground of the era located next to Hammes and the etymology of Badon, we can build a moderately well-represented case that the location of King Arthur's home may once have been found on the summit of Mt Caburn. That is, of course, if we are to believe he existed at all.

Returning to our search for the possibility of a hot spring beneath Old St Peter's, it would now be prudent to examine the evidence concerning the various springs found within a few hundred yards of the church's location at Hamsey.

The previously mentioned Pells Pool (an outdoor swimming pool), found at roughly the same elevation as the bottom of the Hamsey promontory, is fed by a cold-water natural spring to this day. Two additional mapped springs are located at Stoneham Farm on the opposite side of the river and at South Malling. There may even be a further spring beneath Malling Hill that appears to have been concreted over. What we really need to establish in connection to the *Beowulf* text, however, is if a *hot* spring could possibly exist directly beneath the church of Old St Peter's (by the "mounds side").

It took a lot of observation and patience, but one moonlit night in July 2022, I personally witnessed steam rising from a small pool situated at the foot of the bank directly beneath Old St Peter's. I observed this curiosity during an evening spent camping on the opposite side of the river. With further investigation into the activity of this geothermal fault line, I have learned that even in the modern day, the waters in the enormous Roman bathhouse in the city of Bath only rarely steam when conditions allow it. It would appear that the geothermal activity here may have changed somewhat over the centuries. Perhaps these waters were much hotter in the time of the Romans and the Anglo-Saxons, as described in *Beowulf*. Maybe they are largely the same as we find them today, but either way, the likelihood of actually finding a periodically steaming spring directly under the bank of the church, when placed alongside all of the other details I have already provided, is so small, that we are now a long way past the probability of any of this being an unlikely coincidence. I do not doubt that great scepticism will raise its head here, but the picture below is not altered in any way.

The circular pool in the picture below has dried up and subsequently re-appeared over the years. This can be confirmed by looking at historical Google Earth imagery, which has been available since 2004. A further detail to consider is that the great storm of 1287 may have considerably altered the level of the flat ground beneath the bank that we see today. Further silting from subsequent floods throughout the centuries may have also raised the ground level beneath the bank. I would imagine that anywhere up to two or three metres of additional silt may have been added to this flatland by the river since the time of Beornwulf, but even so, it would appear that the same spring still manages to push its way through the earth in precisely the same spot as it always has.

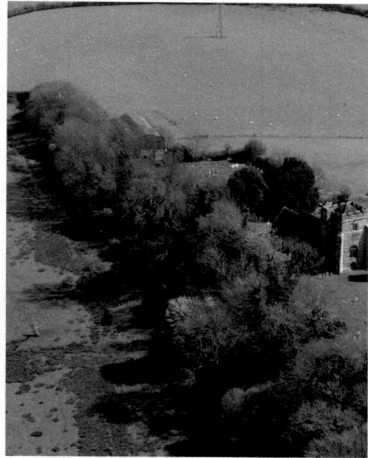

Astonishing as this may already be, we must now continue with the details of the *Beowulf* story and see what else we can discover in relation to the landscape of the Ouse Valley.

"No longer may I here remain. Bid ye men renowned in war to make a mound for me plain to see when the pyre is done upon a headland out to sea. It shall tower on high upon Hronesnaes, a memorial to my folk, that voyagers upon the sea shall hereafter name it Beowulf's Barrow, even they who speed from afar their steep ships over the shadows of the deeps."

> The Beowulf Manuscript
> JRR Tolkien Translation
> Lines 2,352-2,358

We are informed here that Beowulf dies in a location that we have now discovered is called Earnaness and that this location is on a headland "nigh to the watery waves", but subsequently, we are informed that he wishes to be taken *away* from this location to be buried on a different headland "out to sea". So, the question we should ask here is: if he is already on a headland by the sea (as described in the text), why would he want to be taken to another headland by the sea to be buried? If we now acknowledge the situation of Hammes (a headland, once by the sea), we can see that this location is far inland, at the far extremity of the old tidal sea channel. For Beowulf's barrow to be seen by "they who speed from afar their steep ships, over the shadows of the deep'" and "out to sea", the location he wishes to be taken to would *have* to be located somewhere at the head of the coast, on the way into the channel. I would also suggest that whilst a known burial ground is not explicitly mentioned in the *Beowulf* text, perhaps this is the very reason he wishes to be taken there, to be buried with his ancestors. As we will soon see, the situation at Hamsey works perfectly with the two headlands described in the confusing descriptions within the text.

If this supposition is correct, we should now be able to examine further historical and archaeological details contained within the immediate landscape of Lewes, Kingston, and a new location, Telscombe, which can help us add some weight to this possibility. This will subsequently lead us to discover a highly probable location for Beowulf's final resting place.

Our first clue from the *Beowulf Manuscript* is the "Swan Road" or, in other translations, the "Whale Road".

Old English kennings are all of the simple type, possessing just two elements, e.g. for "sea": seġl-rād "sail-road" (Beowulf 1429 b), swan-rād "swan-road" (Beowulf 200 a), bæð-weġ "bath-way" (Andreas 513 a), hron-rād "whale-road" (Beowulf 10), hwæl-weġ "whale-way" (The Seafarer 63 a).

It has long been considered that the Swan Road is simply a reference to the sea. However, if we follow another ancient road from Lewes, past Kingston, and on to a recorded ancient burial ground on the Telscombe Tye, we pass by a small village called Swanborough, previously named "Swanbarrow". This is a recorded settlement during the Anglo-Saxon period and the site of many Anglo-Saxon barrow burials.

So here we are presented with a slight possibility that the "Swan Road" could quite literally be the road that passes by Swanbarrow on the way up to the recorded ancient burial site on the Telscombe Tye. Here, we can find incredible views of the ocean and many surviving barrow burials on the summit of the large hill to this very day. Even if this theory is in error, as an alternative, we could certainly consider the old tidal sea valley of the Ouse itself to be the "Swan Road", as the sea channel would also once have been situated directly beneath Swanborough. Once again, let me also re-state that there is a known ancient burial processional route that exists in Telscombe, and that this is not commonplace.

> **https://www.telscombetowncouncil.gov.uk/wp-content/uploads/2020/10/Telscombe-tye-report-final-docxamededpart.docx-rjm-25march09.pdf**
>
> There is the suggestion that there was a Roman Fort on the Tye and reports of a sunken road used by the Romans to reach their camps. This is likely to refer to the Village Road and Cross Dyke; it was typical that these ancient processional burial routes were used as highways.

Corpse paths worldwide
Wikipedia

A straight Viking cult or Corpse road at Rosaring, Uppland, Sweden, was unearthed by archaeologists. The body of the dead Viking chieftains were drawn along it in a ceremonial wagon to the grave site. The Netherlands had the Doodwegen ("deathroads") or Spokenwegen ("ghostroads"), converging on medieval cemeteries, some surviving in straight section fragments to this day.

"We must hurry now to take a last look at the king and launch him, lord and lavisher of rings, on the funeral road."

The Beowulf Manuscript
Seamus Heaney Translation
Lines 3,007-3,010

From the scant information available on this recorded funeral road, it seems that nobody is certain of the exact course that the route takes, but in the scenario I am presenting, I feel it would be worthwhile to create a link to an additional Anglo-Saxon burial ground which is found at the top of Southover High Street in Lewes. This burial ground is named Saxonbury, and is located mid-way between Hamsey and Telscombe It also dates to the same period as the high-status burial ground beneath Malling Hill, opposite Hamsey.

Curiously and coincidentally, in relation to the "Swan Road", the pub that sits directly adjacent to the Saxonbury burial ground is called the Swan Inn. The junction at which the former burial ground and the pub sit can be reached from Hamsey via one road and from Earwig Corner via another (the river/estuary separates these two locations). From the burial ground at Saxonbury, two routes lead up to the Telscombe Tye. The first route goes straight past Swanborough and then onward to Southease, where the road diverts to Telscombe.

The other possible processional route goes up to the top of the imposing, Castle Hill, after passing through Kingston, then along a ridge of the Downs, and across to the Telscombe Tye. As the journey would have been far easier to make along the road past Swanborough, especially considering that carrying or transporting a bier with a body on it would be no easy task, it seems far more likely that this route would have been used. I suspect that the large valley beneath the current road to Telscombe was *one* of the original funeral roads. As noted in the Corpse paths reference, it is likely that many roads from different settlements would have made their way to one site.

In part two of Martin G Welch's *Early Anglo-Saxon Sussex*, he confirmed the location of the Saxonbury burial ground in Lewes, adding some fascinating details of excavations undertaken there in 1975:

Martin G Welch – Early Anglo-Saxon Sussex Part II
1983
Page 417

1975…

Negative results were obtained in a rescue excavation of the grounds of 'Saxonbury' to the south of the house in advance of road construction (i) and (p). The 32 graves of this cemetery were discovered initially in foundation digging for a house and later in levelling operations prior to laying out a lawn to the east of the house. This house was owned by Mr. Aubrey Hillman, who donated the finds to the Lewes Museum and subsequently named it 'Saxonbury'. It was built in a field immediately north of the Brighton-Lewes railway line and the Sussex Artillery Volunteer Depot and south of a road called 'Mill Road' or 'Juggs Lane'. The excavations were supervised for the Sussex Archaeological Society by Mr B.C. Scammell, who produced the published sketch plans of graves 1-8 (a), and by Mr C.T. Phillips, Hon. Curator of the Society, Mr. E. Cunliffe, Mr. H. Griffith and Mr. J. Sawyer. Graves 1-4 were uncovered in the house foundations (a) and (b), <u>including a skeleton of very tall stature.</u>

The underlined section of the reference above links to a later chapter concerning the probable reality behind "giants" in the Anglo-Saxon period.

It is not known how far the cemetery at Saxonbury extended, but it has been suggested that it stretched far beyond the bend in the road by the Swan Inn, running on beneath Southover Cottage on the other side of the road. As a further remarkable coincidence, this also happens to be one of the houses that I grew up in when I lived in Lewes many decades ago. I only found out about this burial ground 25 years after leaving that house during my research for this book. It is very curious that my research has led me back there.

Leaving those old ghosts behind to continue our list of connections, we will now tackle the name "Hreosnabeorg", which also affords us another clue to the location of Beowulf's burial site.

"Soon was deed of hate and strife betwixt Swede and Geat and feud on either hand across the water wide, bitter enmity in war, since Hrethel was dead, or else the sons of Ongentheow were bold in war, eager to advance, and desired not to keep the peace across the sea, but about Hreosnabeorg (The Whale's Head) they oft-times wrought cruel slaughter in their hate."

The Beowulf Manuscript
JRR Tolkien Translation
Lines 2,076 – 2,081

It is interesting to note that the two other names used in the "kennings" references from *Beowulf* may also relate to the Ouse Valley; "kennings" are described as "allusions that become unintelligible to later generations". The first is "Bath Way", which could be in reference to the bath houses in the valley that we have recently covered. The second is "Whale Road", which is perhaps another name for the road that leads to the Whales Head (Hreosnabeorg), which I am now inclined to believe to be the Telscombe Tye. We will look at the reason for this momentarily.

"No longer may I here remain. Bid ye men renowned in war to make a mound for me plain to see when the pyre is done upon a headland out to sea. It shall tower on high upon Hronesnaes, a memorial to my folk, that voyagers upon the sea shall hereafter name it Beowulf's Barrow, even they who speed from afar their steep ships over the shadows of the deeps."

(Beowulf's dying words)
The Beowulf Manuscript
JRR Tolkien Translation
Lines 2,352-2,358

I have already mentioned that there are many surviving burial mounds on the Telscombe Tye where the referenced ancient burial processional route ends, so with this known burial ground, and its situation by the coast, we have a viable candidate for the location of Hronesnaes.

To add some weight to this theory, another fascinating detail can be found in relation to Brighton/ Beorthelmston, which is in close proximity to the Telscombe Tye. Here, a recorded river once flowed through the bottom of what is now the main high street, which ran inland from the coast. This old waterway, which still flows beneath the road to this very day and frequently gushes out its waters during heavy rainstorms, was once known as the Whalebourne River. Perhaps then, we could infer from this unusual name that the Whales Head may have been located above the Whale's Harbour, which was the entryway into the Whalebourne River. There appear to be no other rivers that share this "whale" name on the entire southern coast (new or old). The proximity of this river to the Telscombe Tye, when considered alongside the reshaping of the southern coastline in 1287, provides us with another noteworthy connection to the *Beowulf Manuscript*.

With all of these tantalising clues leading us to where I

believe Beowulf's burial mound was once located, we must now decipher the most extraordinary details concerning the discovery of what may soon prove to be his actual funerary urn and burned bones. To adequately qualify this incredible possibility, I must briefly jump back into my own story to explain the events that led me to this conclusion.

~ Discovering the Bones ~

After following the descriptive clues I had gleaned from the text and having subsequently located the highest point on the Telscombe Tye, which seemed like a good place to start, it was rather disappointing to find that what had initially looked like an incredibly large burial mound, was actually a large water reservoir created in the early 1900's by a man called Ambrose Gorham. This wealthy horse breeder had brought the first running water supply into the village of Telscombe. However, in a strange twist of fate, the records regarding the creation of this reservoir provided the first clues that marked it out as a possible location for Beowulf's burial mound.

Let's now have a look at the details regarding what this water reservoir was built on top of, and some of what was found in this location prior to its construction.

Telscombe Tye
A report on the historic issues and management by Abbeylands for Telscombe Town Council

Page 2
History

There is evidence of occupation on Telscombe and the Tye since prehistoric times. During excavation of the tumulus on the ancient Cross Dyke for the construction of the underground reservoir, possibly in 1909, three internments were discovered, including a crouched skeleton. In 1922, 23 urns and flints, pieces of burnt bone and shells were discovered, and pottery and cremated bones were unearthed in a wartime trench. There is the suggestion that there was a Roman Fort on the Tye, and reports of a sunken road used by the Romans to reach their camps. This is likely to refer to the Village Road and Cross Dyke; it was typical that these ancient processional burial routes were used as highways.

A tumulus in the Cross Dyke close to the village end was destroyed by the works for the reservoir. A further part of the Cross Dyke, south of the track from Telscombe village county road to Telscombe Road in Telscombe Cliffs, was filled in during the 1970/80s, reputedly by the tenants of the Gorham Trust Property. (*Why would they do this?*) The archaeology remains, however, as the land is not ploughed, and the earthworks are preserved beneath the topsoil. The line of this section of the Cross Dyke is still clearly visible by the remaining scrub and vegetation.

Page 8

A reservoir was constructed in the Cross Dyke, and a part of this Scheduled Monument was destroyed and de-scheduled as a result. Hence, it is in two sections. The management plan of 2002 refers to this and to the improvement of the old Funeral Road, the track running from Telscombe Village to the South Coast Road to bring materials for this construction. In a history of the area on the Saltdean website it refers to this construction being dated 1909, but this is unconfirmed and not supported by other documentary evidence.

I would be interested to know how permission was obtained to destroy a Scheduled Monument in order to build a water reservoir. There is no shortage of space on the summit of the Telscombe Tye, so it appears to have been wholly unnecessary to do so.

The water reservoir with the sea in the background.

For two years, this was the only information I could find on the construction of this water reservoir. Still, even this flimsy record had provided me with some interesting points to examine in relation to the *Beowulf* text.

It states above that three internments were discovered in the tumulus and that one of them was a crouched skeleton. This immediately presented me with a new possibility that had not occurred to me before. Taking note of this information, I went back to the *Beowulf Manuscript* to see if there could be a reference to Beowulf being buried with other people in any of the various translations. Although I could not recall this detail from the countless times I had read and listened to the story, I was astonished to find, that very clearly, the wording of a complete sentence that Tolkien uses does indeed imply that other men were laid in the burial mound alongside Beowulf.

"Now laid they amidmost their glorious king, mighty men lamenting their lord beloved. Then, upon the hill warriors began the mightiest of funeral fires to waken."

The Beowulf Manuscript
JRR Tolkien Translation
Lines 2.632-2,635

Next, I considered that in the text, Beowulf had been cremated in a funeral pyre, so if I had located the correct burial mound on the Telscombe Tye, the crouched skeleton discovered there seemed unlikely to be Beowulf himself. At this stage of my research, I was not even sure if any bones survived after the fires of a funeral pyre, so for a long time, I was left to wonder if this was the correct site and if I would ever be able to know for sure.

Desperately hoping to find out what had happened to the contents of this burial mound, I had not stopped looking for any further information on the excavation but had repeatedly come up with nothing. Then, one fortuitous day, I had a chance encounter with a walker on the trail that led up to the reservoir. Reasonably confident of the many connections I had made between the *Beowulf* text and Hamsey, I had taken to walking up to the site to pay my respects once in a while. If everything I had deduced was correct, then Beowulf/Beornwulf was one of the most remarkable men who had ever lived, and it seemed to me that I may have found his final resting place, but now it had gone. I had grown deeply connected to the *Beowulf* story and the man himself at this stage, so the possible destruction of his burial mound, and the probable loss of the archaeology there seemed like a sad end to such a fantastic story. It appears; however, fate has deemed that the legend of *Beowulf* will never be forgotten.

On my short walk that day, I bumped into and then made friends with a happy dog who was out on his daily walk. Shortly afterwards, I began talking with his owner. This brief encounter then turned into a lengthy conversation which began with a remark I had made about the incredible history of the place we were standing in. This subsequently got me verbally enthused about my research, and still hunting for answers, I mentioned how I was unable to locate any further details on the construction of the reservoir to corroborate any of what I theorised to be true. Incredibly, in a sudden answer to my prayers, this total stranger gave me some fantastic news. It appeared that by chance, he knew of an archaeological report that had been made for Telscombe Church, created during some building work that had been undertaken there some years prior. He also believed that from what he could recall, this report contained some more information on the specific burial mound that I had remarked on.

Immediately, I contacted the church via an email address I found online, and a helpful lady explained that the church was open the following Sunday for a service, and that she would be happy to talk with me that day. Dedicated to the cause, that Sunday, for the first time in many years, I attended an entire church service. When it concluded, I spoke briefly with the churchwarden about an interesting archaeological dig that had been undertaken just outside the church walls and the subsequent archaeological report that was created which might contain the information on the reservoir I was looking for. She kindly agreed to attempt to find it for me, and assured me that if she could locate it, she would send it to me via email. I waited just a few days and, true to her word, she sent it over. The contents of that report were fascinating. Here is the relevant section:

An Archaeological Desk-Based Assessment for St Laurence Church, Telscombe
Page 10

The site of a former barrow (MES2044), which was destroyed in May 1909 during the construction of a reservoir, was situated approximately 350m south of the site. Finds included an 'A' Beaker (the only recorded example from Sussex), with a contracted skeleton and a large "overhanging rim" urn with burnt bones. The Beaker and urn are now in Brighton Museum. No trace of the barrow is left, as the site is now occupied by a reservoir. The location occurs on the line of the ditch belonging to across-ridge dyke, which is discussed below.

From this reference, we find some incredibly exciting additional details to the excavation findings of this barrow.

1. It included an 'A' Beaker with a contracted skeleton.

2. There was also a large "overhanging rim" urn, <u>with burnt bones</u>.

3. The Beaker and urn were in the Brighton Museum!

This was a revelation. Not only were burnt bones and a large overhanging rim urn found in the barrow, but they had also found their way into the Brighton Museum. Could these bones be Beowulf's? It would appear from the article that bones could (and did) survive the fire of a funeral pyre, but also, in this instance, were then collected and placed into an urn. The crouched skeleton or "contracted skeleton" may, therefore, have been one of the "mighty men lamenting their lord beloved", or perhaps a burial from a different era. (I have a strong suspicion that two mounds were excavated there at the same time.)

I then re-examined the *Beowulf* text to see if there were any other details I might have missed regarding an urn in the various translations. In a short time, I discovered the following references, and the puzzle pieces seemed to connect together extremely well:

beadurofes° becn°, bronda° lafe° of [the man] bold in battle, monument (as), of fires, remnant (as)

wealle beworhton°, swa hyt weorðlicost° surrounded (pret 3p), most splendidly

The Beowulf Manuscript
Oxford Press Translation
Line 3,160

"It was their hero's memorial; what remained from the fire they housed inside it."

The Beowulf Manuscript
Seamus Heaney Translation
Line 3,160

It has always been assumed that the mound alone is the referenced monument. Perhaps, however, this "large overhanging rim urn" was also part of that monument, and it, along with the mound, took ten days to create. His burnt bones were then placed inside the urn, and then the urn was placed into the mound.

At this stage, I started to feel that this was all looking very promising in relation to the text, so I contacted the Brighton Museum to see if they still had a fix on the whereabouts of this funeral urn and the burnt bones. Within a few weeks, I got a response. The key details are as follows:

- The reconstructed urn on display in the Brighton Museum is the genuine urn from the barrow on the Telscombe Tye, and the accession number is R933 [HA230017].

- The bones laid out on display by this urn were not from the urn, but the genuine burnt bones from the excavation were stored away safely. Their accession number was recorded as [HA230017.1].

- The urn and bones were handed into the museum in July 1909 by Mr J Johnson M.I.C.E, who, given his membership with the Institute of Civil Engineers, is suspected to have been closely involved in the construction of the reservoir.

- His full address was also included in the email, and his house was in Brighton.

The first point of note was that the burnt bones were safely stored away. The second point of note was that the reconstructed urn was currently on display in the museum which meant I could actually go and look at it, and the third, and most valuable information of all, was the full name and address of the man who had handed in the urn and burnt bones. After deciding to look up this address on Google Maps, I noticed something truly extraordinary. This modest terraced townhouse in Brighton was, *very* unusually, listed as a Bank. Even stranger than this discovery, was that the name of the bank referenced the name of the man who had excavated the burial mound, "Johnson's Bank". Whether this name is in relation to an actual banking facility is not clear at this time and after much deliberation, I have come to the conclusion that it would probably be wise to leave this for others to investigate, but it is certainly another, most curious coincidence.

On a completely unconnected note, let's have a look at these lines from the *Beowulf Manuscript*.

"And they buried torques in the barrow and jewels, and a trove of such things as trespassing men had once dared to drag from the hoard. Let the ground keep that ancestral treasure, gold under gravel, gone to earth, as useless to men now as it ever was."

The Beowulf Manuscript
Seamus Heaney Translation
Lines 3,164-3,168

"In that mound, they laid armlets and jewels and all such ornament as erewhile daring hearted men had taken from the hoard, abandoning the treasure of mighty men to earth to keep, gold to the ground where yet it dwells as profitless to men as it proved of old."

The Beowulf Manuscript
JRR Tolkien Translation
Line 2,650-2,654

It would appear that this sentiment may no longer be valid based on the circumstances we now find. It seems likely that the wonderful hoard of treasure and jewels that may once have been buried there, no longer rests in the ground "as profitless to men as it proved of old". It is not impossible, but it seems unlikely that any of this will ever be confirmed, or that anything that may have come from this mound will ever be recovered, but we do at least have something to work with. If the burnt bones connected to the accession number provided here are located and carbon-dated, we could produce some useful information. The bones should date somewhere between 770 and 830. Let's hope they aren't accidentally lost or tampered with before we get a chance to examine them.

It should also be noted that the curator at the Brighton Museum has stated that the burial mound lost to the reservoir is a Bronze Age burial mound, and that the urn itself is also dated to the Bronze Age. It is, contrarily, currently displayed in the Anglo-Saxon area of the museum directly above a sign that refers specifically to the Iron Age. The urn is also not contemporary with bronze-age designs but rather with known Anglo-Saxon designs. Pictures below:

1. Beornwulf's (possible) reconstructed urn with display bones from the burial mound on the Telscombe Tye.

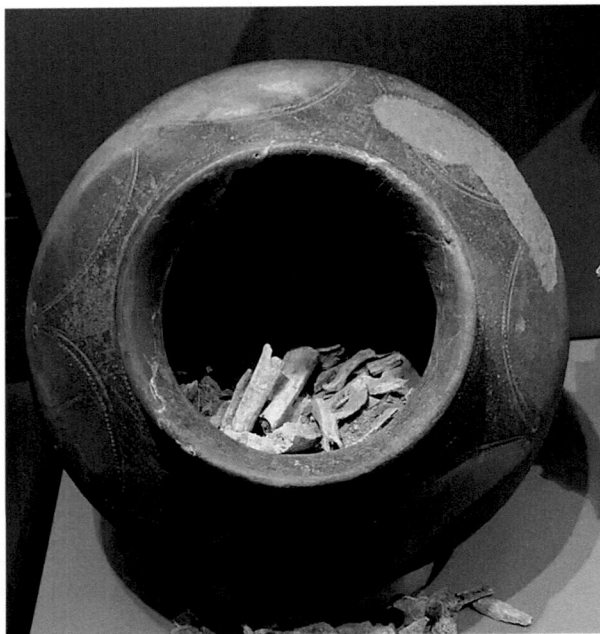

2. Further Anglo-Saxon cremation urn examples.

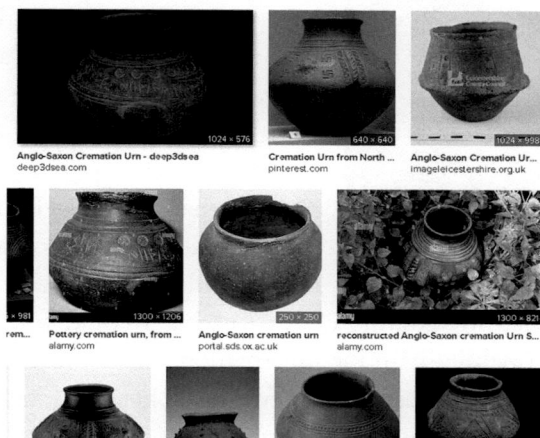

Please note the similar shape and design of the Anglo-Saxon urns in the examples above, and now let us look at what bronze-age cremation urns looked like…

3. Bronze Age burial urns.

As we can see, the curator at the museum is obviously mistaken regarding the dating of this urn and, for some reason, is now unwilling to re-examine it. I requested and offered to pay for the carbon dating of the bones but was informed that they

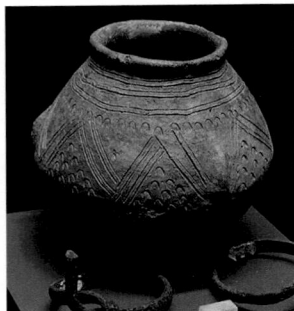

were not able to do it, as two other tests were being undertaken that year. I was not aware that carbon tests carried such a time-consuming workload.

After this disappointing news, I realised that it would be a waste of time attempting to convince this individual to help any further, so I turned my attention back to what I could control, this book. Hopefully, with the information I have presented here, someone at the museum will eventually hear of it and decide to have a look at these bones and the funerary urn with a little more attention to detail; perhaps there is even a complete, identifiable bone that could give us an approximate size for the man. It would be fascinating to discover *precisely* how big this individual was and any further details that analysis could provide.

A final, incredibly personal oddity regarding this burial mound/water reservoir is also worth a mention. During my many hours of research, hunting for any information I could find on its construction, I stumbled across an old record that seemed too strange to be true. In a curious twist of fate, a soldier was stationed at that precise location prior to the Second World War. Sadly, on the 27th of July 1934, an aeroplane crashed right next to the reservoir; its wing then broke off and hit this gentleman with extreme force. He died shortly afterwards from his injuries. This man was called William George. My name is George William Jones. Make of that what you will, but it certainly raised my eyebrow when I found this reference.

OUTLAW

27 Jul 1934

East Sussex Record Office

COR 3/2/1934/66

File

William George of 85 Roman Road, Lowestoft, Suffolk, lamplighter, company sergeant major, 4th Battalion, Suffolk Regiment, Territorial Army; 35; at the Royal Sussex County Hospital, Brighton; cerebral concussion and shock following multiple injuries due to being struck by the wing of an aeroplane whilst engaged as a soldier in the Territorial Army in operations near the Water Tower Reservoir, Telscombe, Sussex; accidental death

Coroner of the Borough of Brighton

Biography [show]

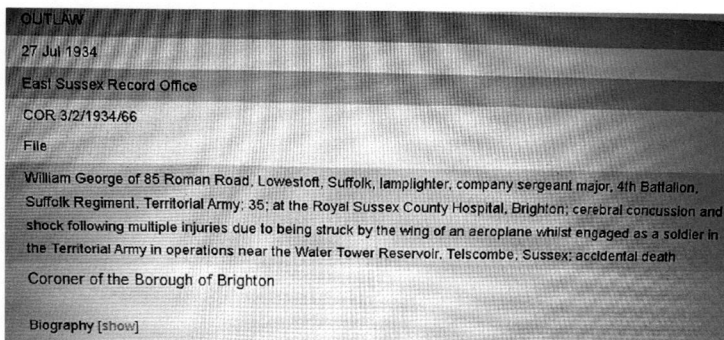

To continue our investigation and to further solidify our findings, we must now tackle one of the most complicated and compelling subjects in the entire *Beowulf* text: the dragon!

~ CHAPTER 12 ~

THE DRAGON

"...until one began to dominate in the dark, a dragon on the prowl from the steep vaults of a stone roofed barrow where he guarded a hoard; there was a hidden passage, unknown to men, but someone managed to enter it and interfere with the heathen trove. He had handled and removed a gem-studded goblet; it gained him nothing, though with a thief's wiles he had outwitted the dragon; that drove him into a rage, as the people of that country would soon discover."

The Beowulf Manuscript
Seamus Heaney Translation
Lines 2,211 – 2,222

aving come this far, and with an ever-growing list of solid connections to the *Beowulf Manuscript*, we must now try to explain the possible reality of the dragon that kills Beowulf at the mouth of the treasure vault. Surprisingly, there is a considerable amount of evidence to cover that will help us to put this subject squarely into the realms of reality. Let us begin with these references from the *Anglo-Saxon Chronicle*, one of which places these serpents directly in Sussex...

Anglo-Saxon Chronicle
Year 774

In this year, the Northumbrians banished their King, Alred, from York at Easter-tide; and chose Ethelred, the son of Mull, for their lord, who reigned four winters. This year also appeared in the heavens a red crucifix, after sunset; the Mercians and the men of Kent fought at Otford; and wonderful serpents were seen in the land of the South Saxons.

Anglo-Saxon Chronicle
Year 793

In this year, terrible portents appeared over Northumbria, and miserably frightened the inhabitants: there were exceptional flashes of lightning, and fiery dragons were seen flying in the air. A great famine soon followed these signs; and a little after that in the same year on 8 January the harrying of the heathen miserably destroyed God's church in Lindisfarne by rapine and slaughter. And Sicga passed away on 22 February.

And now let us look at this initial reference in the *Beowulf Manuscript* in relation to the dragon…

"Even thus had that despoiler of men for three hundred winters kept beneath the earth that house of treasure, waxing strong; until one filled his heart with rage, a man who bore to his liege-lord a gold-plated goblet, beseeching truce and pardon of his master."

The Beowulf Manuscript
JRR Tolkien Translation
Lines 1,916 – 1,920

Our first important detail to examine here is that the dragon has protected this mound for three hundred years. (I am not suggesting that an actual living creature could live for this long, but we will cover the probable reality momentarily.) If we now consider that Beornwulf died sometime around the year 826, and we then remove these three hundred years, we arrive at the year 526. Now, let us look at this reference in the *Anglo-Saxon Chronicle* again for the year 418:

Anglo-Saxon Chronicle
Year 418

Year 418: In this year, the Romans collected all of the treasures which were in Britain and hid some in the earth so that no one afterwards might find them, and some they took with them into Gaul.

If we now acknowledge the possibility that the year 418 was the recorded year that this specific treasure hoard was buried and that the Romans were responsible for it, we have a possible clue for where the *lineage* of the dragon may have come from. In addition, if we refer to the following line in the *Beowulf Manuscript*, we can see that there has been a troop of soldiers left to guard the treasure, and, in the end, only one survives. This is an important detail, as we can now add this soldier's lifespan into the equation, which, at a conservative estimate of 40 years, would bring us to the year 458, or at a non-conservative estimate of 70 years, would bring us to the year 488. Either way, we must now acknowledge the unlikely proximity of these dates. If the author of the *Beowulf* text had written "340 years", the crossover with Beornwulf in the historical time frame of the story would be almost exact. I do not believe that this is an accident. Let us look at the following paragraph again for further information to support this hypothesis...

"There was in that house of earth many of such olden treasures, as someone, I know not who, <u>among men in days of yore had there prudently concealed,</u> jewels of price and mighty heirlooms of a noble race. All of them death had taken in times before, and now he too alone of the proven warriors of his people, <u>who longest walked the earth,</u> watching, grieving for his friends, hoped but for the same fate, that he might only a little space enjoy those long-hoarded things. A barrow already waited upon the earth nigh to the watery waves, new-made upon a headland, secured by binding spells. Therein did the keeper lade a portion right worthy to be treasured of the wealth of noble men, of plated gold; and a few words he spake."

The Beowulf Manuscript
JRR Tolkien Translation
Lines 1,876 -1,888

"Even thus in woe of heart he mourned his sorrow, <u>alone when</u> <u>all had gone</u>; joyless he cried aloud by day and night, until the tide of death touched at his heart."

The Beowulf Manuscript
JRR Tolkien Translation
Lines 1,906 – 1,908

So, with the Romans now in mind, what do we know historically regarding any possible links to rare creatures from around the world? The answer to this question is critical and fascinating...

https://imperiumromanum.pl/en/article/ capturing-wild-animals-in-ancient-rome/

Ancient Romans caught wild animals mainly for the needs of organised games and hunting in amphitheatres (the so-called Venationes). Exotic animals were imported from many lands and provinces, and most often caught by natives who were familiar with their trade and the surrounding area.

Africa was the main source of animal supplies, from where hippos, lions, elephants, giraffes, rhinos and leopards were imported. Tigers were brought from <u>India</u>; interestingly, research indicates that tigers were not only caught in India but also in Armenia. From there, they were transported by sea. Bears, deer, and wild boars were transported from northern and central Europe.

Herein lies an excellent clue to suggest why the Romans may be responsible for the dragon. They are well known for transporting dangerous wild animals all over the world. We also have literary evidence confirming that the Romans brought elephants, lions, and tigers to the shores of Britain. Additionally, we have just learned that many of these animals are caught in Africa and India.

A source for the history of the Hellenistic world and the Roman Republic from 323 to 30 B.C Attalus

When Caesar's passage over a large river in Britain was disputed by the British King Cassivellaunus, at the head of a strong body of cavalry and a great number of chariots, he ordered an elephant, an animal till then unknown to the Britons, to enter the river first, mailed in scales of iron, with a tower on its back, on which archers and slingers were stationed. If the Britons were terrified at so extraordinary a spectacle, what shall I say of their horses? Amongst the Greeks, the horses fly at the sight of an unarmed elephant; but armoured, and with a tower on its back, from which missiles and stones are continually hurled, it is a sight too formidable to be borne. The Britons accordingly with their cavalry and chariots abandoned themselves to flight, leaving the Romans to pass the river unmolested, after the enemy had been routed by the appearance of a single beast.

If we now wish to discover precisely what type of wild animal this "dragon" could be, we must now look at some details of it in the *Beowulf* text, for therein lie many further clues...

"Now the wound that the dragon of the cave had wrought on him began to burn and swell. Swiftly did he perceive that in his breast within the <u>venom</u> seethed with deadly malice."

The Beowulf Manuscript
JRR Tolkien Translation
Lines 2,276 – 2,279

So here we must acknowledge that this dragon, if it is real, is notably poisonous, and that the poison was delivered when Beowulf was bitten by it. So, whatever this creature is, it must have a poisonous bite that produces a burning sensation. It should also be a man-eater.

As a further extraordinary coincidence in relation to Hamsey, there are many legends concerning a type of dragon that is *only* found in Sussex. It is also critical to note that this particular type of dragon from Sussex has the same name as the dragon found in the *Beowulf* text... Let me introduce you now to the curious legends of the knuckers of Sussex...

Knucker
Wikipedia

Knucker is a dialect word for a sort of water dragon living in knuckerholes in Sussex, England. "The word comes from the Old English "nicor" which means "water monster" <u>and is used in the poem Beowulf</u>. It may also be related to the word "Nixie", which is a form of water spirit, to "Old Nick", a euphemism for the devil, or to the words "Nykur" (Icelandic water horse), "Nickel" (German goblin), "Knocker" (Cornish goblin), "Näcken" and "Neck" (Scandinavian water men and water spirits), "Näkineiu" and "Näkk" (Estonian mermaid and singing water animal), and "Näkki" (Finnish water spirit).

In the following reference from an old newspaper article, we find further descriptive details of a "Nicor" or "Knucker" within an extraordinarily recent account from 1614 of a dragon sighting in a town called Horsham. In this article, we are given further descriptions that match with the details we have on knuckers, along with some additional, vital information. Notably, Horsham is also in Sussex and provides us with a further etymological link to the Anglo-Saxons. Horsham may derive from "Horsa", "Horsa's Ham" (Hengest and Horsa), who is also mentioned in *Beowulf*.

---

http://www.sussexarch.org.uk/saaf/dragon.html

TRUE AND WONDERFUL

A Discourse relating a strange and monstrous Serpent (or Dragon) lately discovered, and yet living, to the great Annoyance and divers Slaughters both of Men and Cattell, by his strong and violent Poyson. In Sussex, two miles from Horsam, in a Woode called St. Leonards Forrest, and thirtie miles from London, this present month of August, 1614. With the true Generation of Serpents.

"In Sussex, there is a pretty market-towne, called Horsam, neare unto it a forrest, called St. Leonard's Forrest, and there, in a vast and unfrequented place, heathie, vaultie, full of unwholesome shades, and over-growne hollowes, where this serpent is thought to be bred; but, wheresoever bred, certaine and too true it is, that there it yet lives. Within three or four miles compasse, are its usual haunts, oftentimes at a place called Faygate, and it hath been seen within halfe a mile of Horsam; a wonder, no doubt, most terrible and noisome to the inhabitants thereabouts. There is always in his tracke or path left a glutinous and slimie matter (as by a small similitude we may perceive in a snaile's) which is very corrupt and offensive to the scent; insomuch that they perceive the air to be putrified withall, which must needes be very dangerous. For though the corruption of it cannot strike the outward part of a man, unless heated into his blood; yet by receiving it in at any of our breathing organs (the mouth or nose) it is by authoritie of all authors, writing in that kinde, mortall and deadlie, as one thus saith.

"Noxia serpentum est admixto sanguine pestis. – LUCAN"

This serpent (or dragon, as some call it) is reputed to be nine feete, or rather more, in length, and shaped almost in the forme of an axeltree of a cart; a quantitie of thickness in the middest, and somewhat smaller at both endes. The former part, which he shootes forth as a necke, is supposed to be an elle long; with a white ring, as it were, of scales about it. The scales along hist backe seem to be blackish, and so much as is discovered under his bellie, appeareth to be red; for I speak of no nearer description than of a reasonable ocular distance. For coming too neare it, hath already beene too dearly payd for, as you shall heare hereafter.

It is likewise discovered to have large feete, but the eye may be there deceived; for some suppose that serpents have no feete, but glide upon certain ribbes and scales, which both defend them from the upper part of their throat unto the lower part of their bellie, and also cause them to move much the faster. For so this doth, and rids way (as we call it) as fast as a man can run. He is of Countenance very proud, and at the sight of men or cattel, will raise his necke upright, and seem to listen and looke about, with great arrogancy. there are likewise on either side of him discovered, two great bunches so big as a large foote-ball and (as some thinke) will in time grow to wings; but God, I hope, will (to defend the poor people in the neighbourhood) that he shall be destroyed before he grow so fledge.

He will cast his venome about four rodde from him, as by woefull experience it was proved on the bodies of a man and a woman comming that way, who afterwards were found dead, being poysoned and very much swelled, but not prayed upon. Likewise a man going to chase it, and as he imagined, to destroy it with two mastive dogs, as yet not knowing the great danger of it, his dogs were both killed, and he himselfe glad to returne with haste to preserve his own life. Yet this is to be noted, that the dogs were not prayed upon, but slaine and left whole: for his is thought to be, for the most part, in a conie-warren, which he much frequents; and it is found much scanted and impaired in the encrease it had woont to afford.

These persons, whose names are hereunder printed, have seene this serpent, beside divers others, as the carrier of Horsam, who lieth at the White Horse in Southwarke, and who can certifie the truth of all that has been here related.

John Steele.
Christopher Holder.
And a Widow Woman dwelling nere Faygate

Assuming we accept this report as the truth, it has provided us with some fascinating particulars. If we now include the other descriptions we have of "Knuckers", we can subsequently produce a detailed list of features for this mystery creature of Sussex:

- It can swim.
- It is about 9ft in length.
- It has a long neck.
- It has large feet.
- It resembles the axle tree of a cart.
- It is poisonous/venomous and kills by it.
- It leaves behind a glutinous, slimy matter.
- It lives in a rabbit (conie) warren.
- It is a man-eater
- It sometimes stands arrogantly upright, surveying its surroundings.
- It has a putrid scent that it leaves behind.
- It has football-like protrusions on its side.
- It has a white stripe near its head.
- It lives near strange pools that are infinitely deep.

Now that we have all of these descriptive details, it is finally time to tell you what, in all likelihood, this creature really is. The only way I feel that I can present this and for you to believe the truth of it, is to show you now, point by point, that every single feature I have listed above (as described by the legends and articles provided) can only be found in one creature on planet earth – the Komodo dragon. It is critically notable here that this lizard is also one of the only creatures on earth that still bears the name "dragon". This is unlikely to be an accident, for we also have another reference that supports this very theory. One of the oldest surviving maps of the world was drawn on an ostrich egg. On that globe is a notation above the area that we now know as Komodo Island. The notation reads... "hic sunt dracones"... (here are dragons).

Here are dragons
Wikipedia

Until the Ostrich Egg Globe was offered for sale in 2012 at the London Map Fair held at the Royal Geographical Society, the only known historical use of this phrase in the Latin form "HC SVNT DRACONES" (i.e., hic sunt dracones, 'here are dragons') was the Hunt-Lenox Globe dating from 1504. Earlier maps contain a variety of references to mythical and real creatures, but the Ostrich Egg Globe, and its twin, the Lenox Globe are the only known surviving globes to bear this phrase. The term appears on both globes at the peripheral, extreme end of the Asian continent.

Now, let us confirm beyond doubt *all* of the descriptive points listed above with pictorial evidence to back this proposition up. Subsequently, we can look at how the Romans may have documented this creature using a different name that many of us may be familiar with from the recent fame (in the scheme of things) of JK Rowling's, *Harry Potter*.

1. Let's start with the first four points, which we can strike off the list with one picture…

It can swim.
It is around nine feet in length.
It has a long neck.
It has large feet.

2. It looks like the axel-tree of a cart…

3. It is poisonous/venomous and kills by it…

https://www.nationalgeographic.com › animals › article › komodo-dragon-venom

Research Finds That Komodo Dragons Kill With Venom – National Geographic

Komodo dragons kill using a one-two punch of sharp teeth and a venomous bite, scientists have confirmed for the first time. The find dispels the common belief that toxic bacteria in the Komodos…

4. It leaves in its trail a glutinous slimy matter…

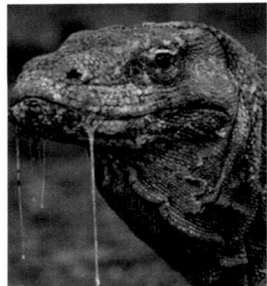

5. It lives in a rabbit/coney warren…

Additionally, the females ensure that their nest is deep (e.g., 2 meters into the ground). The deepness creates an ideal environment for the eggs with stable temperatures and sufficient moisture.

6. It is a man-eater…

https://www.rusticaly.com/komodo -dragons-eat-humans/

Komodo Dragons Eat Humans • Here's What People Don't Know

Komodo Dragons Eat Humans • Here's What People Don't Know: A person can be killed by Komodo dragons in a matter of hours. The <u>Komodo dragon is one of the most venomous reptiles in the world.</u>

7. It sometimes stands arrogantly upright, surveying its surroundings...

Komodo dragons have poor eyesight
They assume this posture to sniff, or taste the air, when hunting for prey.

8. It has a putrid scent that it leaves behind...

Besides staying in trees, baby komodos also cover themselves in adult komodo feces.

The feces musk their scent and keep adult Komodos away from them.

9. It has football-like protrusions on its side.

Komodo dragon after eating large prey whole.

10. It has a white stripe near its head.

Some immature
Komodo dragons have
white stripes near their
heads.

11. It lives near strange pools that are infinitely deep.

Komodo dragons are exothermic animals and like to wallow
in hot springs. Connected to underground fault lines, this is
likely the reason that the springs in Sussex were perceived

as being infinitely deep. The steam they produced may also have been thought of as smoke by the people of the Anglo-Saxon era. Below is an article that would strongly support this supposition:

https://www.atlasobscura.com /places/slayers-slab

Knucker

The knucker, named for the Saxon nicor, or water monster, is an aquatic dragon-like creature, said to have its lair in the nearby pool, synonymously named the Knucker Hole. Thought to be bottomless, this hole swallowed a cord of six of the church's bell ropes that had been tied together, and still its bottom was not found. The Knucker Pool is now on private land and inaccessible throughout most of the year, in the past however the water from its pool was said to cure all ills – if one was brave enough to get so close to the Knuckers abode, that is. The water is not only famed for its medicinal value, but also for the fact it never freezes, some say this is because of the fact it is fed by a fast-moving underground spring, shielded from freezing air, while others believe this is due to the warmth of the Knucker's fiery breath.

To continue with this hypothesis, we must now consider how Komodo dragons may have first been acquired, and then subsequently brought to the shores of Britain. The answer to this is found in one of the most significant Roman ruins ever discovered. This ruin is in the southern tip of India, directly adjacent to Malaysia and an island chain that runs straight to Komodo Island. The proximity of these locations is the most likely answer to the question of how Komodo dragons were first discovered, and then how they subsequently made their way over to the shores of Britain.

Arikamedu: Ancient Roman Site in India
https://factsanddetails.com/india/History

Arikamedu, an Early Historic Site (near Pondocherry on the east coast of southern India), was nominated to be a UNESCO World Heritage site as one of the Silk Road Sites in India in 2010. According to a report submitted to UNESCO, Arikamedu is one of the biggest ancient Roman trade centres in India (approximately 34 acres). Unlike many other Roman trade centres including those on India's Malabar coast, Arikamedu has been properly identified and is to a large extent, well-documented. The site of Arikamedu enjoys the distinction of being the first site in the whole of India to provide evidence, through archaeological digs, for the export of variety of Indian objects, viz Glass beads, Shell, Terracotta objects, besides Muslin cloths. Most of the other Roman trade sites of India have been dated on the basis of the chronology of Arikamedu. [Source: Archaeological Survey of India]

Let us now continue with this possible Roman connection to the Komodo dragon and look at what Pliny the Elder wrote about something called a "basilisk" in his book, *Natural History*, written around 79 AD.

Pliny the Elder's Natural History

There is the same power also in the serpent called the basilisk. It is produced in the province of Cyrene, being not more than twelve fingers in length. <u>It has a white spot on the head, strongly resembling a sort of a diadem.</u> When it hisses, all the other serpents fly from it: and it does not advance its body, like the others, by a succession of folds, <u>but moves along upright and erect</u> upon the middle. It destroys all shrubs, not only by its contact, but those even that it has breathed upon; it burns up all the grass, too, and breaks the stones, so tremendous is its noxious influence. It was formerly a general belief that if a man on horseback killed one of these animals with a spear, <u>the poison</u> would run up the weapon and kill not only the rider, but the horse, as well. To this dreadful monster the effluvium of the weasel is fatal, a thing that has been tried with success, for kings have often desired to see its body when killed; so true is it that it has pleased Nature that there should be nothing without its antidote. The animal is thrown into the hole of the basilisk, which is easily known from the soil around it being infected. The weasel destroys the basilisk by its odour, but dies itself in this struggle of nature against its own self.

Adolescent Komodo Dragons, one with a white diadem marking on its head. Immature Komodo Dragons like these would have been easier to capture and transport.

As described above in relation to the basilisk, Komodo dragons are also known to hiss. So, as we can now see above, every single description of the Knucker fits perfectly with the only creature on earth to carry *all* of these characteristics. This reptile is also named a "dragon" in the earliest references available to us. The probability that this is all entirely coincidental seems too unlikely to be true when we consider the eras in which these references were documented and the sheer number of correlating facts we are presented with. It is also notable that when examining ancient paintings of knights battling dragons, they are mostly depicted as the exact size and roughly the same shape as a Komodo dragon; they are rarely depicted as flying or as monstrously large creatures.

Coming back to how a lone dragon could have possibly survived for three hundred years, we should know that in the real world, it could not. What we *can* say is that Komodo dragons produce many offspring and are even capable of asexual reproduction. One Komodo dragon can produce upwards of twenty eggs per year without the need for a male of the species to fertilise them. It would seem far more likely that there was not one lone dragon but possibly hundreds of them alive over the course of the centuries, descendants of the first of their species to have been brought to Britain. In a reference we will look at very soon, we read that "Sussex was *infested* by Serpents of an enormous size." Not a lone serpent, but an *infestation* of Serpents. It would, in all likelihood, be more accurate to state that the Komodo dragon *species* lived in these lands for three hundred years. This multiple dragon hypothesis would also make a lot of sense in relation to the story of Ragnar Lodbrok. We will cover this Ragnar/Beowulf connection in full, in a separate chapter.

With so many perfect descriptive connections to the

dragon now confirmed, this is the most probable truth on the matter of these dragons. In relation to *Beowulf*, let us also remember that the "nicor" is the specific dragon species documented in the manuscript, adding further weight to our previous findings. We still, however, have not explained how these creatures were perceived to be flying, and the incredibly obvious answer is that they were not...

"Burning, woeful at heart, ofttimes he compassed all the circuit of the mound, but no man was there in the waste. Nonetheless he thought with joy of battle, of making war. Ever and anon he turned him back in to the barrow, seeking the jeweled vessel. Quickly had he discovered this, that someone among men had explored the gold and mighty treasures. In torment the Guardian of the Hoard abode until evening came. Then was the keeper of the barrow swollen with wrath, purposing, fell beast, with fire to avenge his precious drinking-vessel. Now was the day faded to the serpent's joy. No longer would he tarry on the mountain-side, but went blazing forth, sped with fire."

The Beowulf Manuscript
JRR Tolkien Translation
Lines 1,930 – 1,942

From this reference, we have another critical detail: the dragon circles his mound during the day and waits until darkness arrives before flying through the night. A further line explains that come the morning, the dragon retreats to his lair...

"Back to his Hoard he sped to his dark hall ere the time of day."

The Beowulf Manuscript
JRR Tolkien Translation
Line 1,950 – 1,951

This dragon, then, for whatever reason, *only* flies at night. To answer the question of why that would be important, we need to examine some important events that occurred during the years surrounding the life of Beornwulf. Hidden away in these historical records are details recorded for an extraordinary phenomenon; it is called a Miyake event...

Miyake Event
Wikipedia

A Miyake event is a powerful burst of cosmic rays. The origin and cause of these increases in cosmic ray activity is currently unknown. The outbreaks are marked in particular by the increase in the radioactive Carbon isotope 14C in tree rings, <u>meaning the events can be dendrochronogically dated</u>. Given their recent discovery, the number of confirmed Miyake events is relatively low (5 or 6 events); hence, their periodicity remains unknown. However, some initial models estimate that one such event would take place once every 400-2400 years. The currently known Miyake events took place <u>around</u> 7176 BCE, 5410 BCE, 5259 BCE, 663 BCE, <u>774-775 CE</u> and 993-994 CE. According to a study conducted by a University of Queensland team led by astrophysicist Benjamin Pope, some of the events were short-lived, <u>while others lasted for years</u>. A Miyake event occurring in the near future, as interpreted by various scientists, would have significant impacts on global technological infrastructure such as satellites, telecommunications, and power grids.

Anglo-Saxon Chronicle
Annus Domini, the year of the Lord 774

In this year, the Northumbrians banished their King, Alred, from York at Easter-tide; and chose Ethelred, the son of Mull, for their lord, who reigned four winters. <u>This year also appeared in the heavens a red crucifix, after sunset</u>; the Mercians and the men of Kent fought at Otford; and <u>wonderful serpents were seen in the land of the South Saxons</u>.

The "red crucifix" recorded by the *Anglo-Saxon Chronicle* has been variously hypothesised to have been a supernova or the <u>aurora borealis</u>.

In the *Anglo-Saxon Chronicle* reference above, we have details of a red crucifix in the heavens (after sunset). It would seem highly likely from these historical references and the descriptions we have in the *Beowulf* text that this Miyake event phenomenon is what both the author of Beowulf, and the *Anglo-Saxon Chronicle* are referring to. The people of the time must have conflated the two occurrences: the Miyake event producing aurora borealis during the night, and the additional sighting of real-life "wonderful serpents" (Komodo dragons) in the land of the South Saxons. When the sun rose each morning, the aurora borealis were no longer visible; thus, the dragon "sped back to his lair". The fact that the largest solar flare event in recorded history occurred within fifty years of the death of Beornwulf, coupled with all of our other findings, seems like too much of a coincidence to dismiss. Perhaps further, smaller events occurred during the mid-820s, creating more aurora borealis phenomena in the skies above Sussex. The *Anglo-Saxon Chronicle* entry for the year 793 we have previously looked at would suggest that this is highly probable.

Anglo-Saxon Chronicle
Year 793

In this year, terrible portents appeared over Northumbria, and miserably frightened the inhabitants: these were exceptional flashes of lightning, <u>and fiery dragons were seen flying in the air</u>. A great famine soon followed these signs; and a little after that in the same year on 8 January the harrying of the heathen miserably destroyed God's church in Lindisfarne by rapine and slaughter. And Sicga passed away on 22 February.

It will be challenging to prove any of this unequivocally, but it appears to be too much of an unlikely coincidence for the dating of these aurora occurrences and the dragon of *Beowulf* only flying at night, not to be connected. If we then consider the sheer number of correlations we have already found between the story and the historical record that are real and observable, then this is the most likely answer to explain the reality behind the legend of these dragons.

A further reference (below) also places these serpents directly in Lewes, from a publication called *Ancient and Modern Lewes and Brighthelmston*. The date of this reference, the year seven hundred and seventy-four, is also the exact year stated for the Miyake event.

Ancient and modern Lewes and Brighthelmston
Page 30
Saxon Annals – (Chronicle of Mallros)

"In the year seven hundred and seventy four, <u>Lewes and other parts of Sussex</u>, are said to have been infested by serpents of an enormous size. For this I can cite but one authority, and that not the least apocryphal among the quaint volumes of monkish history. Neither can I relate from it what mischief the serpents did, nor how the country was cleared of them."

I am sure that the question of how a Komodo dragon could have survived in England will rear its head among the sceptics. The answer to this is in the location that they are found within Britain. Notably, there are no legends concerning Knuckers beyond the south of England. The probable reason for this comes in the form of the geothermal hot springs that we have now discovered are scattered throughout this region of Britain and are heavily linked to the legends of Knuckers.

Atlas Obscura Online
Slayers Slab Reference

The Knucker, named for the Saxon nicor, or water monster (from which the devil's name Old Nick also derives), is an aquatic dragon-like creature, said to have its lair in the nearby pool, synonymously named the Knucker Hole. Thought to be bottomless, this hole swallowed a cord of six of the church's bell ropes that had been tied together, and still its bottom was not found. The Knucker Pool is now on private land and inaccessible throughout most of the year, in the past however the water from its pool was said to cure all ills- if one was brave enough to get so close to the Knuckers abode, that is. <u>The water is not only famed for its medicinal value but also for the fact it never freezes</u>; some say this is because of the fact it is fed by a fast-moving underground spring, shielded from freezing air, while others believe this is due to the warmth of the Knucker's fiery breath.

There appear to have been numerous hot springs in the areas surrounding Lewes, other springs that stretched over to the famous Roman bathhouse in Bath, along with further springs that exist all the way over to Wales. We have also discovered that these hot springs are all connected via an underground fault line that runs through the South of Britain. If we then acknowledge that the Knuckers are famously documented as living by "knuckerholes" (deep pools of warm water), we can begin to understand how they would have been able to stay warm during colder weather. We have also learned that the Komodo dragon makes its lair up to two metres below the ground precisely so that it can maintain a steady temperature. As exothermic animals, it is likely that this is why they were only found in the South of England, and why they were so commonly associated with knuckerholes.

It is also worth noting that we do not know precisely how hardy these reptiles truly are. Alligators can survive below-zero temperatures for months on end thanks to a process known as brumation. I suspect that during the colder months in England, Komodo Dragons would have spent much of their time in brumation or full hibernation. Existing today on islands in Indonesia, they do not need to hibernate as the temperature remains steadily within a range that they find comfortable. Other lizard species in colder climates, however, are known to hibernate through the colder months. It seems very probable that Komodo dragons would be capable of quickly adapting to a new environment and would seek out the warmest habitat they could find to survive the winter. We must also not forget that if the Romans had brought these creatures over, at least initially, they would have attempted to look after them and keep them alive for their games or circuses. Perhaps the "Venationes" purposely housed them around the hot springs of Sussex in an effort to keep them alive and comfortable. I have also considered the outlandish possibility that these serpents were used as a type of "guard dog" by the Romans to protect their valuables. Perhaps this use eventually led Komodo dragons to become associated with treasure hoards in myth and legend.

In concluding this chapter on dragons, I would briefly like to consider an additional folk story from Mayfield in East Sussex, which may also be curiously related to these serpents...

Village.Net
Mayfield Reference

Mayfield is famous for the legend of St Dunstan. The saint, formerly a blacksmith, was working at his forge when the Devil paid him a visit, disguised as a beautiful woman, with a view to leading him astray. However, St Dunstan spotted the cloven hooves beneath the dress, and grabbed the devil's nose with his red-hot pincers! thus foiling Satan's evil intentions. According to another legend, Satan returned again as a weary traveller in need of a horseshoe, Dunstan saw through the disguise once again and beat the Devil until he pleaded for mercy, and swore never to enter any house with a horseshoe above the door. Not surprisingly, the church is dedicated to St Dunstan.

It is set back from the main street and was largely rebuilt after a fire destroyed it, along with most of the village, in 1389. It was damaged again in 1621 when it was struck by lightning. The importance of the iron industry (Roman) in the area is seen again inside the church, where two cast iron tomb slabs are set in the floor of the nave.

Dunstan became Archbishop of Canterbury <u>from 960 – 988</u> and is credited with founding Mayfield Palace near the church. It was one of the great residences of the medieval Archbishops of Canterbury. It ceased to be an ecclesiastical residence and was sold off in 1567.

***

Having lived in Mayfield for the better part of seven years, I was always fascinated by the legend of St Dunstan and often wondered about its origins. It seemed to be a strangely detailed myth that made very little sense. However, my research into the legends of the Knuckers has curiously provided me with a loose theory. Let's look at this reference in detail once more...

Knucker is a dialect word for a sort of water dragon, living in knuckerholes in Sussex, England. "The word comes from the Old English "nicor" which means "water monster" and is used in the poem Beowulf. It may also be related to the word "Nixie", which is a form of water spirit, to "Old Nick" (Nicor), <u>a euphemism for the Devil.</u>

Here, we have a reference that relates the knucker to Old Nick, "a euphemism for the Devil". We then have the curious detail of St. Dunstan grabbing the Devil by the nose with a pair of iron tongs. So, as strange as this story already is, why would anyone decide to grab a human "Devil" by the nose? This seems like an extraordinary thing to do (even to the Devil), but quite possibly, not so strange if a moderately immature Komodo dragon wandered into the village one day. To stop it from biting him, perhaps St. Dunstan squeezed some tongs over its nose and mouth and then killed it or led it out of town. Maybe the story was elaborated on over the years, evolving slowly from a Nicor to Old Nick and then to the Devil himself. We can also see from the legend that St. Dunstan is alive in the century directly after the rule of Beornwulf, so we can loosely connect the phenomena of Nicor dragons, their locations, and the eras in which they appear active together. I have no idea how much truth there is to this further musing of mine, but if this legend truly has its roots in a historical event, it seems an awful lot more likely that my interpretation of the myth occurred as opposed to the actual Devil wandering into Mayfield dressed as a woman, who then proceeded to let himself be grabbed on the nose by iron tongs, which somehow disabled him completely.

There is one further curiosity concerning dragon origins to consider, and perhaps some evidence that could be obtained to support the Komodo dragon hypothesis. I will not explore it too much here as I do not have access to the artefacts or information that could provide me with the answer.

Gideon Mantell, the "Godfather of Dinosaurs", is a famous (previously discussed) palaeontologist from Lewes who, as fate would have it, discovered the teeth and some fragments of bone belonging to something that has now been deemed to be from the Jurassic period. The various teeth and bone fragments he located were considered to have come from a giant lizard, and this new dinosaur was named Iguanadon. Despite the reportedly large tooth size, it would probably be a good idea to check that these Iguanadon teeth are not, in fact, Komodo dragon teeth. Without access to any original pictures of them, I cannot comment any further, but from the images I have been able to find of their skeletons, the similarities in these two creatures' physical make-up are stunning, and to reiterate once more, the bones and teeth were found somewhere in Sussex. Gideon Mantell lived in Lewes, right next to Hamsey.

It is also worthwhile to learn that the *two* versions of the story concerning where he found these teeth are oddly conflicting. This seems somewhat strange in itself. One version tells us that the bones and teeth were discovered in a chalk pit on Malling Hill by workmen who first discussed the finds with Gideon Mantell's wife; the next day, he went to the chalk pit himself and procured the finds from the workmen. The second story is that he found them in Cuckfield.

As a very last, unimportant but particularly strange coincidence, I would like to share with you the name that I recently discovered for an extremely rare protected orchid species currently found on the Hamsey promontory… It is called the Lizard Orchid.

GRENDEL'S MOTHER DRAGS BEOWULF TO THE BOTTOM OF THE LAKE

~ CHAPTER 13 ~

GRENDEL & ANGLO-SAXON GIANTS

The subject of Grendel, the first "monster" that Beowulf battles with, is far more elusive than the dragon when it comes to literary evidence. The long and short of it is that there is very little information to help us along the way, either in the *Beowulf* text, or in any figures we have in our historical records. What we *can* say about Grendel, however, is that far from only being described as a monster, it is a critical fact that within the *Beowulf Manuscript*, Grendel is also described as a man...

"Thus the troop-men lived agreeably, at ease, until a certain one began to perpetrate crimes, a hellish foe; the unyielding demon was named Grendel, a well known wanderer in the wastes, who ruled the heath, fen, and fastnesses; the ill starred man had occupied for some time the habitat of monstrosities, after the Creator had cursed him among the race of Cain- the eternal Lord was avenging the murder after he killed Abel; he derived no satisfaction from that feud, but Providence <u>banished him</u> far away from humankind on account of that crime."

The Beowulf Manuscript
RD Fulk Translation
Lines 99 – 111

This detail is important when we consider how Grendel is portrayed today. As with the dragon, current media productions present him as a creature that is not of this world, but as we can see in the reference above, this is not the case. What little information we do have would place this man squarely in the realms of reality. It seems likely that these descriptions are telling us that this man is a skogarmaor, a berserker, or both.

https://vikings.fandom.com/wiki/Skogarmaor
Skogarmaor | Vikings Wiki | Fandom

A Skogarmaor (meaning "man of the forest"), also called útlagi (meaning "outlaw"), is a Norse outcast who has been <u>banished</u> from their community for various crimes. Full outlawry was also called skóggangr (meaning "going into the forest").

https://www.britannica.com/topic/berserker
Berserker
Norse warrior

Berserker, Norwegian berserk, Old Norse berserkr ("bearskin"), in premedieval and medieval Norse and Germanic history and folklore, a member of unruly warrior gangs that worshipped Odin, the supreme Norse deity, and attached themselves to royal and noble courts as bodyguards and shock troops.

The berserkers' savagery in battle and their animal-skin attire contributed to the development of the werewolf legend in Europe. It is unclear whether the berserker warriors <u>wore bear and wolf skins into battle</u> or fought bare-chested (i.e., without byrnies or mail shirts); tapestries and other sources represent both possibilities. The berserkers were in the habit of raping and murdering at will in their host communities (thus going "berserk"), <u>and in the Norse sagas they were often portrayed as villains</u>. In an Old Norse poem, most of which dates from the 9th century, berserkers are recorded as the household guard of Norway's King Harald I Fairhair (reigned 872–930)

———————————————————————

The next obscure link to the possible reality of Grendel comes to us in the form of a place named Rendelsham in East Anglia. This has loosely been attributed to an Anglo-Saxon man named Rendel. However, I have begun to seriously consider the possibility that this name has either *devolved* from Grendelsham (Grendels Ham) to Rendelsham, or that the name Grendel *evolved* from Rendel. It is unknown who the ruler of East Anglia was during the life of Beornwulf, but perhaps in one scenario, we could consider Grendel to have been a savage, giant warlord who was outcast from his home and who then became a Viking raider/berserker. Later, at some point during his life, he settled or conquered lands in East Anglia and raided from the coast there. Perhaps Hrothgar was targeted by him specifically because his lands and society were precisely where Grendel was originally outcast from.

This initially seems like a thin hypothesis, but two additional connections to Rendelsham help to support this theory. The first is that Rendelsham is located next to Woodbridge in Suffolk. Woodbridge is the location of the famous Sutton Hoo ship burial where an Anglo-Saxon king, who is thought to be Readwald, was discovered. With wonderfully preserved finds made during the excavation, we were provided with one of the first pieces of physical archaeology that related explicitly to the *Beowulf* text and provided our first physical clue to support the case for its historical basis. It came to us in the form of the Sutton Hoo helmet and the boar-shaped cheek pieces that were discovered on it. This exact description was given to us of this precise helmet design in the *Beowulf* text:

"Boar shapes flashed above their cheek-guards, the brightly forged work of goldsmiths, watching over those stern faced men."

The Beowulf Manuscript
Seamus Heaney Translation
Lines 303-306

Bizarrely, the next unusual connection to the possible reality of Grendel comes in the form of a well-documented UFO sighting witnessed in Rendelsham Forest, which has strange connotations to the mere lands that Grendel lives in...

The Rendelsham Forest Incident
Wikipedia

The Rendlesham Forest incident was a series of reported sightings of unexplained lights near Rendlesham Forest, in Suffolk, England, in late December 1980, which became linked with UFO landings. The events occurred just outside RAF Woodbridge, which was used at the time by the United States Air Force. USAF personnel, including deputy base commander Lieutenant Colonel, claimed to see things they described as a UFO.

The occurrence is the most famous of UFO events to have happened in the United Kingdom and is among the best-known reported UFO events worldwide. It has been compared to the Roswell UFO incident in the United States and is sometimes called "Britain's Roswell".

The U.K. Ministry of Defense has stated that the event posed no threat to national security, and therefore, it was never investigated as a security matter. Sceptics have explained the sightings as a misinterpretation of a series of nocturnal lights: a fireball, the Orfordness Lighthouse, and bright stars.

"A few miles from here a frost-stiffened wood waits and keeps watch above a mere; the overhanging bank is a maze of tree-roots mirrored in its surface. <u>At night there, something uncanny happens; the water burns</u>. And the mere bottom has never been sounded by the sons of men. On its bank, the heather-stepper halts: the hart in flight from pursuing hounds will turn to face them with firm-set horns and die in the wood rather than dive beneath its surface. That is no good place. When wind blows up and stormy weather makes clouds scud and skies weep, out of its depths a dirty surge is pitched towards the heavens. Now help depends again on you and on you alone. Seek it

**if you dare. I will compensate you for settling the feud as I
did the last time with lavish wealth, coffers of coiled gold,
if you come back."**

(Description of Grendel's Mere)
The Beowulf Manuscript
Seamus Heaney Translation
Lines 1,362 – 1,379

I must state here that for this interpretation to be correct,
Hrothgar, Heorot and Grendel would need to be placed
in East Anglia, which contrarily, I do not believe to be the
case. For my part, I believe that the available evidence would
place Hrothgar and Heorot in Gotland, which is a small
island between Denmark and Sweden (we will cover this
fully in a later chapter). However, I can only postulate from
the information I have at hand, and these three links seem
strangely connected. Perhaps the lights seen in Rendelsham
forest are connected to the previously discussed geothermal
activity of the time and are, in turn, connected to further
hot springs located in this area or maybe even in Gotland
itself. This seems to be a moderately accurate reflection of
the description in the *Beowulf* text. The possibility certainly
warrants further investigation, and it will be interesting to see
if anyone can make any sense of it. One particularly well-
considered theory suggests that flammable gases can rise from
decaying matter in swampy landscapes, which spontaneously
combusts when it comes into contact with oxygen-rich air,
creating burning orbs of light. These have been given many
names over the centuries, including Will O The Wisps and
Jack O Lanterns.

The final worthwhile possibility for placing the existence
of the enormous monster, Grendel, into the realms of
reality, comes to us in the form of living "Giants" from

the Anglo-Saxon period. The actual, current definition of a giant to this day, is a human being that is over seven feet tall:

https://tallsome.com/how-tall-considered-giant
How Tall to Be Considered a Giant – Tallsome

To be considered a giant, you need to be 7 feet (2.20 cm) or taller. Gigantism is caused by an over-production of growth hormones.

With this real-world definition, we have many examples of living giants among the human population that are alive today. It is a known fact that some of these individuals are suffering from a form of gigantism, but it is also acknowledged that some other individuals are genetically *"true"* giants and are naturally very large human beings. These individuals have been well-documented across the world. Here is an example of one man from the U.K.:

United Kingdom

236 cm

7 ft 9 in

Angus MacAskill

Tallest "true" giant (not due to a pathological condition). 1825–1863 (38)

This is interesting in relation to both Beowulf *and* Grendel, as the text repeatedly gives the clear impression that both individuals are far stronger and larger than ordinary men.

"Seafarers who ferried the gifts of the Geats here to our satisfaction used to say that he, brave in war, had the strength of thirty men in his hand-grip."

The Beowulf Manuscript
RD Fulk Translation
Line 374

"It was not allowed him that the blade of any weapon of iron could help him in battle; the hand was too strong that, I have heard, overtaxed with its stroke every sword whenever it bore to battle a weapon hardened in wounds, he was none the better for it."

The Beowulf Manuscript
RD Fulk Translation
Line 1682

If we then consider that the average height of an ordinary man in the 800s would have been around 5 feet 5 inches tall and that 7 feet (plus) "giants" existed but were a rarity in the Anglo-Saxon period, it is easy to imagine how those individuals would have been perceived by the rest of the population living alongside them. The sheer size difference would also have given a larger, sword-wielding warrior an incredible advantage on the battlefields of the time, marking them out as people to be both feared, documented, and remembered.

We are also fortunate enough to have evidence of recorded skeletons of true giants that date to the Anglo-Saxon period. This allows us to place them directly in the lands of Britain at precisely the right time to further support this Grendel hypothesis.

http://frontiers-of-anthropology.blogspot.com/2014/
03/skeletons-of-dark-age-european-giants.html

Skeletons of Saxon Giants Over 7 feet tall: 6th & 7th centuries A.D.

At least two notable gigantic skeletons of Saxon men, towering 7 feet to 7 feet 4 inches tall, have been documented from 6th and 7th century A.D. Saxon graves in the 20th century at two independent sites in Northern and Eastern Britain.

First is the "Burgh Castle giant." On Display in the Royal Ontario Museum in 2012 (Apparently no longer on display as of Oct. 2013). Acquired in 1967 – 68, this skeleton was found near a Roman Fort in a 7th century Saxon Castle in Norfolk, England. The height of the man was approximately 7 feet 4 inches (2 m, 23) and his age was around 40 years at death.

The original article on the Burgh Castle Giant is from a book titled *Pathologically Speaking* by Janet Cooper. It was written in 1977. The full description is on page 37 and confirms that this giant is a true giant. At the time of writing, the article is available online.

This record confirms that the genetic trait of true giants was alive and present during the correct period for our investigation. It is easy to imagine how these enormous individuals would likely have been both feared and venerated above the ordinary folk of the day. I suspect many of these giant men would have become kings or warriors by simple force or perhaps, even by election due to their superior physical stature. It would appear that this is what the following reference from the *Beowulf Manuscript* is speaking of regarding Beowulf's ancestor, Beow.

"Afterwards a boy child was born to Shield, a <u>cub</u> in the yard, a comfort sent by God to that nation. <u>He knew what they had tholed</u>, the long times and troubles they'd come through without a leader; so the Lord of Life, the glorious Almighty, made this man renowned. Shield had fathered a famous son: Beow's name was known through the North."

The Beowulf Manuscript
Seamus Heaney Translation
Lines 12 – 19

If we then consider the possibility that Grendel or "Rendel" was another warrior of extraordinary size, yet perhaps smaller than Beowulf himself, we can begin to formulate a more likely scenario for a plausible reality regarding the details of the fight between Beowulf and Grendel at the great hall, Heorot. Curiously, no weapons are used, and the battle ends when Beowulf rips Grendel's arm off, creating the wound that will eventually kill him. It is worth considering here that the fight details may also have been exaggerated somewhat over the countless retellings of the story, along with the size of the dragon, but who knows, maybe he was strong enough to rip Grendel's arm off, and perhaps the arm really was hung above the door of the hall. We may never know the exact truth of these details.

The last link to the possible reality behind the legend of Grendel presents itself to us in the macabre form of cannibalism. It is historically documented that in the time of Wilfred (600s) and Beornwulf (800s), the inhabitants of England and Scandinavia were starving populations. We are informed today that in the time of Wilfred, these early

Saxon warrior tribes had not learned the art of fishing. In my estimation, this seems highly unlikely and would suggest a certain amount of Christian propaganda. Crops, however, were undoubtedly harder to grow in the northern regions of the world. We are led to believe from current research that one of the most important and probable reasons for the Vikings attempting to settle on the shores of Britain came in the form of a requirement for good farmland and better growing conditions. If starvation occurred in the Scandinavian region, as the historical records suggest, we can imagine the horrors that may have occurred as a result of hard famine and how this may also support the idea of a cannibalistic man named Grendel during this era. We should additionally consider the genuine phenomena of "Chinese Whispers" or "Telephone" in the US. This is an important reality to consider with regard to the subsequent interpretation of the monster, Grendel, and is without a doubt, a common culprit for many of the blurred distances we now find between the actual events of history and surviving myths.

There is one further, undeniable factor that we should take into account, and that is *drama*. When it comes to spinning a good tale, the old saying, "Why let the truth get in the way of a good story?" springs to mind. Essentially, people tend to enjoy exaggeration and drama, so storytellers eventually deliver this to them.

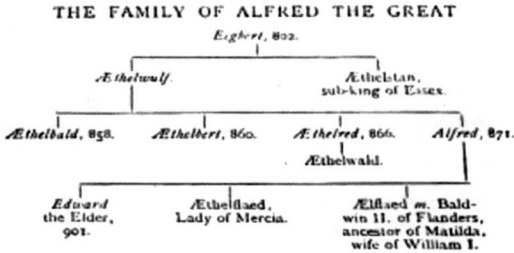

Egbert, 802.

Æthelwulf.   Æthelstan,
                                              sub-king of Essex.

Æthelbald, 858.   Æthelbert, 860.   Æthelred, 866.   Alfred, 871.
                                      Æthelwald.

Edward   Æthelflaed,   Ælflaed m. Bald-
the Elder,   Lady of Mercia.   win II. of Flanders,
901.   ancestor of Matilda,
                                       wife of William I.

~ CHAPTER 14 ~

THE BEOWULF MANUSCRIPT AND THE EARLY ANGLO-SAXON KINGS

Now that we have made multiple points of contact with the *Beowulf Manuscript* and have subsequently connected them to the landscape of Sussex, the Clofesho witans, and the historical characters of Beornwulf and Wiglaf, it is time to tackle some incredible possibilities in relation to who some of the other characters in the text may be. By no means, with regard to this chapter, is anything categorically proven to be true. These are simply my considerations, given the correlating information I have pieced together so far from the observable links between the *Beowulf* text, the landscape of Sussex, and the documented Anglo-Saxon royal family of Wessex and Mercia during the period that surrounds the reign of Beornwulf, which all matches up *exceptionally* well.

Below, we have a pertinent paragraph in relation to this topic from the introduction to the *Beowulf Manuscript* by RD Fulk:

That Beowulf had grown obscure by the time it was copied into the extant manuscript is demonstrated by the sorts of errors committed by the scribes, especially in the copying of proper names, which, it is apparent, were often entirely unfamiliar to the copyists. That such a lengthy poem, full of puzzling allusions to a vanished world and of no obvious ecclesiastical use, should have been copied at about the millennium is thus perhaps the greatest wonder presented by this book of many wonders.

The Beowulf Manuscript
RD Fulk (Introduction)
Page 25

As a first point, the reference above confirms the critical premise that many names within the text contain errors committed by the scribes and that these names were often entirely unfamiliar to the copyists.

It is important to note that in one particular line of the *Beowulf Manuscript*, Beowulf himself is described as an "aetheling". This is a critical detail, as this word is a title that is usually reserved for the son of a king in Anglo-Saxon England and nowhere else. From this one simple word then, we could imply that Beowulf is <u>recognised in the text</u> as the son of an Anglo-Saxon king.

"Gloomy was his spirit though, death-eager, wandering; the weird was at hand that was to overcome the old man there, seek his soul's hoard, and separate the life from the body; not for long now would the <u>athelings</u> life be lapped in flesh."

The Beowulf Manuscript
Michael Alexander Translation
Lines 2,415-2,421

The word "aethel" is relatively unique to the Anglo-Saxons, and it is noteworthy that this word is recorded in the *Beowulf Manuscript* in its original form, "aethelinges". This is another big clue concerning Beowulf's true origins, and it also makes further sense if we now look at some striking correlations between the English royal family from the era that the historical Beornwulf lived in, and the additional characters found within the *Beowulf* text.

We should start with Beowulf's father in the manuscript; he is called Ecgtheow...

> **Beowulf, <u>Ecgtheow's son</u>, replied: "Well, friend Unferth, you have had your say about Breca and me."**
>
> *The Beowulf Manuscript*
> *Seamus Heaney Translation*
> *Lines 529-531*

It is a critically important observation that there are *no* other characters in the *Beowulf* text with a name beginning with Ecg. If we then consider the possibility that Beowulf is indeed Beornwulf, could there be any other characters from Beornwulf's period that also have a name beginning with Ecg? The answer to this is yes, and there is only one: Ecgberht. We have already discovered, in chapter three, that King Ecgberht was fighting either with or against Beornwulf at the battle of Ellendun in the year 825. So, here we have an immediate crossover. Beowulf and Ecgtheow and Beornwulf and Ecgberht are, in both instances, alive at the same time.

Now we must continue with this premise and see if there is any way to create a more plausible, solid connection between the two characters, Ecgberht and Ecgtheow. First of all, we must examine the names themselves. Let us start with Ecgberht, for, as with many of these modern interpretations of old names, this is not how his name was originally documented. Ecgberht is first recorded as Ecgbeorht.

If we examine the name Ecgtheow of the *Beowulf Manuscript* and reverse engineer the "th" section, which was the Anglo-Saxon letter "thorn", which looks similar to a "b", we end up with "Ecgbeow". So now we have two names, far closer to their original spelling, that are incredibly similar: "Ecgbeow" and "Ecgbeorht". "Ecgbeorht" is the spelling most commonly used on Ecgberht's coinage. We have already discussed the connection between Beorht and Beorhthelmston (Brighton) and the subsequent connections to the Clofesho witans, possibly in Hammes, with Beornwulf presiding as King. If this deduction regarding Ecgtheow is correct, then it is utterly astonishing, as we will shortly discover that our historical King Ecgberht is actually the <u>step</u>father of Beornwulf. Or, to put it another way, as described in the *Beowulf* text, Ecgtheow is the father of Beowulf.

So, if Beowulf was really the *<u>stepson</u>* and not the *<u>son</u>* of Ecgtheow, he would have to have married Ecgtheow's daughter, and this detail is actually available to us in the text...

His father, long dead now, was Ecgtheow titled,
<u>Him Hrethel</u> the Geatman granted at home his
One only daughter, his battle-brave son.

Translates to...

His Father, long dead now, was titled Ecgtheow,
He, the High Noble ('<u>Hrethel</u>' etymology) of the Geatmen,
<u>granted at his home</u> (to Beowulf)
<u>His only daughter, to his battle-brave son. (son in law)</u>

Let's look at these sentences a little further, as other translations state: "<u>To</u> him, Hrethel the Geatman granted at his home..." This is an absolutely critical wording choice, as each version completely changes the identity of Hrethel. With the "Him Hrethel" translation, we are being informed that King Ecgtheow is Hrethel. With the "To him, Hrethel" translation, we are being told that Hrethel is a completely different person from Ecgtheow. Given the multiple correlating characters to follow, "Him Hrethel" would now appear to be the correct translation. Ecgtheow *is* Hrethel.

From our surviving historical sources, we do not know if King Ecgberht had a daughter, as it is not recorded today. It would seem highly probable, however, that a king of his era would undoubtedly have had more than one child and that any one of them could have been female. The family tree presented at the beginning of this chapter points to the existence of *two* sons of Ecgberht, one of which is called Aethelstan. Whoever this particular Aethelstan may have been, even he is no longer recorded as Ecgberht's son, but we *are* informed that Aethelwulf, Ecgberht's known son, *did* have a son called Aethelstan. From the matching details to follow regarding the recorded sons of Hygelac in the *Beowulf Manuscript*, I would hazard an educated guess that Aethelstan is more likely to be a son of Ecgberht.

Returning to a possible daughter of Ecgberht, sadly, written evidence for female offspring is lacking for nearly all of the early chronicled kings. This does not mean, however, that those kings only had sons; but rather that female offspring during these centuries were largely irrelevant to the chroniclers as they were not in the line of accession.

It seems possible to me now that Beornwulf may have been born in Sussex (Geatland) but maintained strong ancestral ties to Denmark (Gotland), conquered or became a part of a society in the south of Sweden, and eventually married a daughter of Ecgberht, King of the West Saxons.

If we wish to add some more weight to these interesting parallels, we should now be able to place further connected characters from the *Beowulf* text lineages into the known historical lineages we have for Ecgberht and his family, as in each case, we are provided with both. Concerning this, we must remember that different nations have different names for the same characters in history. To further confound the senses, we must also acknowledge the extraordinary amount of variation in the documented spelling of each name. In the case of Ecgberht alone, we have six different versions, and perhaps even seven if we now include "Ecgtheow".

Ecgberht, King of Wessex
Wikipedia

Ecgberht (770/775 – 839), also spelt Egbert, Ecgbert, Ecgbriht, Ecgbeorht, and Ecbert, was King of Wessex from 802 until his death in 839. His father was King Ealhmund of Kent.

Important characters reference:

> *"Beowulf, son of Ecgtheow, spoke: "Many a skirmish I survived when I was young and many times of war: I remember them well. At seven, I was fostered out by my father, left in the charge of my people's lord. King Hrethel (Ecgtheow) kept me and took care of me, was open handed, behaved like a kinsmen. While I was his ward, he treated me no worse as a wean about the place as one of his own boys, Herebeald and Haethcyn, or my own Hygelac. For the eldest, Herebeald, an unexpected deathbed was laid out, through a brother's doing when Haethcyn bent his horn*

tipped bow and loosed the arrow that destroyed his life. He shot wide and buried a shaft in the flesh and blood of his own brother."

The Beowulf Manuscript
Seamus Heaney Translation
Lines 2,425-2,440

From this reference, we find some noteworthy information: Beowulf is fostered out to Hrethel by his biological father, who, as I now understand it, is *not* Ecgtheow. Hrethel (who *is* Ecgtheow) has three other sons: Herebald, Haethcyn and Hygelac. Hygelac is described as "my own" in relation to Beowulf, so here we are being led to understand that somehow, Hygelac is more closely related to Beowulf. It seems likely to me, from the information that I have now deciphered, that Hygelac is Beowulf's stepbrother (as previously noted) and that "my own" may relate to a special bond of friendship rather than that of family by blood. Other examiners of the text have proposed that Hygelac is Beowulf's uncle. If the historical Ecgberht is indeed "Ecgtheow", and Hygelac is the *son* of Hrethel (Ecgtheow), does Hygelac bear any similarity to Aethelwulf, King Ecgberht's recorded son?

As I have noted, in our surviving historical sources, Ecgberht's known, recorded son and heir is a man called Aethelwulf. Hidden away in the details of Aethelwulf's life, we are fortunately given some noteworthy, matching information for the character Hygelac within the *Beowulf* text. This parallel between the historical record and the *Beowulf Manuscript* relates to the two characters' wives.

We are told historically that during his life, Aethelwulf married a girl named Judith who then became queen, and notably, that she was only twelve years old at the time of their marriage. So, if Aethelwulf is indeed a different name for "Hygelac", does this information regarding his wife match with the description of Hygelac's wife in the *Beowulf* text?

> *"Not far thence must they go to find <u>Hygelac Hrethel's son</u> giver of rich gifts, where he dwelleth in his own house, chief amid his champions, nigh to the walls of the sea. Good was that mansion, a brave king was its lord, lofty were his halls; <u>very young was Hygd, wise and of virtue seemly, though winters few she had known within the castle courts,</u> Haereth was her sire."*

> The Beowulf Manuscript
> JRR Tolkien Translation
> Lines 1,611-1,619

Here, we have been presented with a further possible connection for identifying Hygelac as Aethelwuf, in the noted details concerning the two characters marrying noticeably young wives (Hygd and Judith).

It is worthwhile at this junction to also learn that in the group of original books that include the *Beowulf* text, the book that follows directly after *Beowulf* is called *Judith*. This is far too complicated a subject to examine here, however. (This is certainly confusing enough!)

These details alone are still not enough to be certain that this is entirely correct, so now let us see if there are any further connections to the historical figure of Aethelwulf (Ecgberht's recorded son) that we can parallel with the characters in the *Beowulf* text.

Below is an important article regarding the current information we have available on the descendants of Aethelwulf...

Aethelwulf
Wikipedia

Æthelwulf's father, Ecgberht, was King of Wessex from 802 to 839. His mother's name is unknown, and he had no recorded siblings. He is known to have had two wives in succession, and so far as is known, Osburh, the senior of the two, was the mother of all his children. She was the daughter of Oslac, described by Asser, biographer of their son **Alfred the Great**, as "King Æthelwulf's famous butler", a man who was descended from Jutes who had ruled the Isle of Wight. Æthelwulf had six known children. His eldest son, **Æthelstan** (*remember here that Aethelstan on the family tree above, was once ascribed to Ecgberht*), was old enough to be appointed King of Kent in 839, so he must have been born by the early 820s, and he died in the early 850s. The second son, **Æthelbald**, is first recorded as a charter witness in 841, and if, like Alfred, he began to attest when he was around six, he would have been born around 835; he was King of Wessex from 858 to 860. Æthelwulf's third son, **Æthelberht**, was probably born around 839 and was King from 860 to 865. The only daughter, **Æthelswith**, married Burgred, King of Mercia, in 853. The other two sons were much younger: **Æthelred** was born around 848 and was King from 865 to 871, and **Alfred** was born around 849 and was King from 871 to 899. In 856, Æthelwulf married Judith, daughter of Charles the Bald, King of West Francia, and future Carolingian Emperor, and his wife Ermentrude. Osburh had probably died, although it is possible that she had been repudiated. There were no children from Æthelwulf's marriage to Judith, and after his death, she married his eldest surviving son and successor, Æthelbald.

It is important to note here that apart from Alfred, the prefix to all of the names of Aethelwulf's children is "Aethel", which translates directly to "The noble", so we have the father, Aethelwulf "The Noble Wulf", and his children: The Noble Stan, The Noble Berht, The Noble Red, The Noble Bald, and for Aethelwulf's only daughter, The Noble Swith, and lastly, Alfred. Curiously, the name Alfred is derived from Alf (Elf) and Raed (Council). "Elf Council".

So, the identifying part of these names (apart from Alfred) are the suffixes attached to the end of "The Noble". This is important when we now look at further characters in the *Beowulf Manuscript* that are connected to Hygelac's (or Hrethel's) children. As I have suggested, I am proposing that Hygelac is a title used for Aethelwulf and that Hrethel is a title used for Ecgberht. Hrethel etymologically derives from Hr-<u>aethel</u>. As we have just discovered, Aethel translates to "The Noble". I now wonder if this name relates to "The leader of the Nobles" as "Hygd" etymologically translates to "Thoughtful, Comforter, Considerate"; titles rather than known names.

It is interesting to note here that the name "Hygelac" has, in the opinion of modern historians, lent some credibility to the historical basis for *Beowulf*. The Hygelac that they are referring to is actually from the 520s, however, and this does not fit with even the most optimistic of early dating for the events of *Beowulf*. It seems far more likely that many of these names have been used repeatedly through generations, as we have already seen with the multiple "Beo" names we covered in chapter eight, and that the Hygelac (Aethelwulf) of the *Beowulf* text is actually from the late 700's, with a shared title from a common ancestor. There is also a strong possibility that Hygelac is a further descriptive title, used by the scribe who penned *Beowulf*. On one line of the original manuscript, it

states: "ofer yþa° gelac°", which translates to "of the waves".
It seems likely that Hygelac equates to "Ruler of the Waves".

*"Across the wide sea, desolate and alone, the son of Ecgtheow
(Beornwulf) swam back to his people. There Hygd (Judith)
offered him throne and authority as lord of the ring-hoard:
with Hygelac (Aethelwulf) dead, she had no belief in her son's
ability to defend their homeland against foreign invaders.
Yet there was no way the weakened nation could get Beowulf
(Beornwulf) to give in and agree to be elevated over Heardred
(Aethelred) as his lord or to undertake the office of kingship."*

The Beowulf Manuscript
Seamus Heaney Translation
Lines 2,367-2,376

Here, we have been given the name of Hygelac's son and
successor at this stage in the story of *Beowulf*; he is called
Heardred. So now we have another match. One of Aethlwulf's
six known children is "The Noble Red", so here, Heard-red
could be referring to Aethel-red.

It is almost impossible to decipher definitively who is
related to whom, but the further names we are provided in
relation to Hrethel's sons are strikingly similar to the further
proposed sons of the historical King Aethelwulf. This does
not quite fit with the *Beowulf Manuscript* in that we are told
there that these matching children's names belong to Hrethel
(Ecgberht) and <u>not</u> to Hygelac (Aethelwulf), his son. The
similarity in all of these names is so striking, however, that
it should not be ignored. It is all <u>incredibly</u> confusing, but it
seems statistically unlikely that *all* of these characters from
Beowulf would have names and information that match up so
well to *all* of the royal family from only one, incredibly brief
period of history which happens to surround the lives of

the historical Beornwulf, Ecgberht, and Aethelwulf.

Despite the fact that some of these names are documented multiple times throughout the *Anglo-Saxon Chronicle,* pertaining to further historical kings, at no point other than in the time of Ecgberht, Aethelwulf, and Beornwulf do we find the whole group of name connections pertaining to the *Beowulf* text. Historically, we can also be certain that Aethelwulf's reign coincides precisely with Beornwulf's reign. Perhaps someone will work out the intricacies of this baffling conundrum sometime in the future. I suspect that many of these sons are misattributed either in the *Beowulf Manuscript* or in our historical documents. It is also perfectly possible that some of the names and translated associations within the text were copied down in error, as highlighted by Professor RD Fulk. As an immediate example, we have been informed historically that (as far as is known) all of Aethelwulf's children are from his first wife, Osburgh, but even this seems improbable. I would suggest (as was curiously depicted in the TV series *Vikings*), that Judith is likely the mother of some of these children.

I have now provided us with information to connect Ecgtheow (Hrethel) to Ecgberht, Hygelac to Aethelwulf, Hygd to Judith, Beowulf to Beornwulf, Wiglaf to Wiglaf, and Heardred to Aethelred. So now let us look at the final three relatives of this family that are discussed in the *Beowulf Manuscript*: Herebeald, Haethcyn, and possibly, the eldest "Yldestan"- Aethelstan.

Herebeald

The second son of Aethelwulf, **Æthelbald**, was King of Wessex from 858 to 860. Aethelbald usurped the throne from his father Aethelwulf when he chose not to relinquish control of the throne on his father's return from a pilgrimage to Rome. On the death of Aethelwulf, he is also thought to have married his stepmother, Judith (Hygd).

Haethcyn

Haeth Cyn, (etymologically), "King of the wasteland" or perhaps, <u>famously</u>, Alfred the Great, the fifth son of Aethelwulf.

Æþelwulf (c.795 – 858)

Genealogy. https://www.geni.com/people/ Aethelwulf-king-of-Wessex/6000000003826814612

Alfred was born around 849 and was King from 871 to 899. In 856, Æthelwulf married Judith, daughter of Charles the Bald, King of West Francia, and future Carolingian Emperor.

A user from the United Kingdom says the name Haeth is of English origin and means "Anglo-Saxon Old English word for Heath (wasteland)".

A user from New York, U.S., says the name Haeth means "Home/wasteland".

2. According to a user from Colorado, U.S., the name Haeth is of Welsh origin and means "Wilderness".

https://ifunny.co/picture/the-english-term-king-comes-from-the-anglo-saxon-term-4ngPbqGL9

The English term "King" comes from the Anglo-Saxon term "cyning" from cyn or kin, and -ing meaning "son of ". As Kings of that time always held hereditary titles.

Aethelstan

Yldestan – the "eldest". The eldest son of Aethelwulf (or Ecgberht).

"For the eldest a bed of murder was spread unfittingly by the actions of his kinsman, one brother the other, with a bloody dart."

The Beowulf Manuscript
Seamus Heaney Translation
Lines 2,425-2,440

This has been translated as a reference to Herebeald in the story, but it may be incorrect. It would be interesting to see how the word Yldestan is spelled, if the line can be construed in a different manner, and if the "Y" is capitalised in the original manuscript. If this is correct, it would mean that King Alfred may have either purposefully, or accidentally, killed his own brother (Aethelbald or Aethelstan).

From this connection, (if it is correct), we may also be able to deduce some further lost details regarding the unknown events behind King Alfred's death, directly from the *Beowulf Manuscript*.

Current information on the death of King Alfred

Read More: https://www.grunge.com/235346/the-mysterious-death-of-alfred-the-great/

Just because you're King and roundly lauded as Great doesn't mean there won't be mysteries around your life and, for that matter, your death. There doesn't seem to be any consensus about what prompted Alfred to join the Choir Invisible. New World Encyclopedia relates that even the King's death date is disputed – October 26, 899, but only probably. "How he died is unknown," we're told. "He had suffered for many years from a painful illness," gastrointestinal in nature, that would sometimes confine him to his rooms for days or even weeks at a time with cramps and diarrhoea. Some historians speculate Alfred suffered from Crohn's disease, says History Hit – an "inflammatory bowel disease," says The Mayo Clinic, that's "painful and debilitating" and can lead to malnutrition and even death – perhaps even Alfred's, which would not be so great. But nobody knows for sure.

Remember at Ravenswood, Ongentheow slaughtered Haethcyn, Hrethel's son when the Geat people in their arrogance first attacked the fierce Shylfings.

(The Death of Alfred the Great?)
The Beowulf Manuscript
Seamus Heaney Translation

If accurate, this implies that King Alfred was a son of Ecgberht,

"Him, Hrethel". This should be Hygelac's (Aethelwulf's) son if it were to fit into our current historical record. Either could be wrong.

Hrethelings
Wikipedia

Beowulf's author uses the term 'Hreþling' to refer to the descendants of Hreðel and to Hygelac in particular.

Hrethling means "the son of the high noble" and is likely to be the Danish version of the Old English "aethling".

I feel it is important at this point to reiterate the introduction to the *Beowulf Manuscript* by RD Fulk.

"That Beowulf had grown obscure by the time it was copied into the extant manuscript is demonstrated by the sorts of errors committed by the scribes, especially in the copying of proper names, which, it is apparent, were often entirely unfamiliar to the copyists."

(Introduction)
The Beowulf Manuscript
RD Fulk
Page 25

I hope you have followed at least some of this information. I cannot explain how difficult this chapter has been to put together. It was just as confusing for me to write as it probably has been for you to read, but I do believe that these name connections and etymological parallels will stand up well to close examination by any detail-related research enthusiasts. It should, I hope, also excite some interesting rhetoric among historians with any further information that could connect to this theory.

Below is a list of 13 characters that I have examined from the *Beowulf Manuscript* and who I now believe they relate to in our historical records, all from precisely the same period:

Beowulf – Beornwulf

Wiglaf – Wiglaf

Ecgtheow – Hrethel etymology ("The High Noble") – Ecgberht

Hygelac – Aethelwulf

Hygd – etymology ("The Thoughtful, Comforter, Intelligent") – Judith

Haereth – Charles the Bald

Heardred – Aethelred

Herebald – Aethelbald

Haethcyn – etymology ("King of the Heath / Wasteland") – Alfred

Hrothgar – Hemming (See next chapter)

Halfdane – Halfdane

Wulfgar – Wulfgar

The Frankish King – Charlemagne

And now let us come full circle with this new information and see if we can connect Alfred the Great (Haethcyn) to Lewes Castle, from a publication in the 1800s which contains information that is no longer available to us in any recorded form, but was once proposed here:

INTERNET ARCHIVE

24

TALES AND REAL

LEWES CASTLE, AND THE PRIORY OF ST. PANCRAS.

WITH A SHORT ACCOUNT OF THE LEGEND OF LEWES CASTLE.

OME writers, especially Grose, state that Lewes Castle was originally built by Alfred the Great, after his victory over the Danes in the year 884. When the crown of England was wrested from the brow of the brave but unfortunate Harold, at the battle of Hastings, in 1066, the rape of Lewes fell, in the appointment of the Conqueror, the lot of William de Warrenne, a knight of the court of Normandy; who, by his marriage with Gundreda, fourth daughter of William the Conqueror, had the tie of relationship to strengthen the claims of a successful warrior. This castle was entirely neglected after the death of the eighth Earl of Warrenne, in 1307, and in the year 1440 it had altogether ceased to be accounted of any value. In 1774 the site and ruins were leased by the lords of the barony for ninety-nine years to an ancestor of the present holder. The keep has been judiciously repaired by the present owner; and from its battlements the visitor cannot fail to be highly gratified with the prospect before him. A spacious bowling-green has been formed within the base-court,

Sadly, there appears to be no surviving recorded reference for the claim made here by Grose, which states that the castle was built by Alfred the Great. This does not mean, however, that it is not true. In a detailed examination of this claim, Thomas W Horsfield and Gideon Mantell (both antiquarians of Lewes) worked together and produced a publication called *The History and Antiquities of Lewes and its Vicinity*. The following paragraph provides a most convincing argument for the true reality behind this proposition, stating that, in all probability, there was a castle at Lewes in the time of Alfred, long before the arrival of William Warenne and its later reconstruction.

It must also be noted that there appears to be an enormous hole in the surviving Anglo-Saxon records for Sussex. Other researchers have also noticed the curious lack of information available for the county during this era. It is known and documented that King Alfred ordered the repair and fortification of Burghs (fortified encampments) in Sussex to protect his lands from the invading Great Heathen Army, but

The true statement of the case is probably the following :—In the Saxon times a castle was built here, comprehending within its walls the elevated area of the castle banks, and extending to the extremities of the scite on which the two mounts stand. When William de Warren received from the Conqueror the grant of the barony and castle of Lewes, the old fortification was taken down. The two extremes of the long diameter of the area, were divided from the rest by a deep and broad fosse, and with the materials thrown from the fosse, the two elevated mounts were raised, upon each of which a fortification or keep was constructed; and the whole surrounded by a strong embattled wall, strengthened with turrets, or towers at certain distances, at the base of which was dug a broad and deep fosse.

sadly, there is no further record to be found on this subject. I strongly suspect that much of this information may have been destroyed during the fire at Ashburnham House, where the *Beowulf Manuscript* and other important documents were discovered. We do, however, have the references that link King Alfred to the Battle of Ashdown and Terrible Down, both of which are in the near vicinity of Lewes.

Failing the future discovery of some lost *Anglo-Saxon Chronicle* in another library somewhere, which at this stage seems highly unlikely, we can only guess at what remarkable information they could have contained. Given the situation of Lewes and the connections to the Anglo-Saxons that we have already made within the Ouse Valley, it seems highly probable that he did build a Burgh there. Geographically, at the very least, it would be incredibly challenging to create a convincing argument that implied he would *not* build defences there. The East and South Coast of England would clearly have been significant locations within the country. This is where many sailing vessels coming from Sweden, Norway, Denmark, and France would all have once arrived at. As a useful early navigation tool, this specific piece of ancient coastline in Sussex would also be easy to locate as it is marked out by the Seven Sisters cliff formation. To this very day, the main shipping routes to England are found at Dover and Newhaven. Newhaven Harbour leads *directly* to Hamsey and Old St Peters Church. If you needed an easy meeting place (Clofesho) to navigate to, Hamsey would have been a perfect choice.

QUEEN WALTHEOW & BEOWULF

~ CHAPTER 15 ~

HROTHGAR & HEOROT

With all of the connections we have made to the story so far, there is one further investigation we must also now consider: the location of Hrothgar and the great hall, Heorot. We have already ascertained that this location is in Danish lands and that an ocean must be crossed to get there. As previously noted, an additional and critical detail is that the precise duration of the journey from Geatland to Heorot is also recorded in the *Beowulf Manuscript*; we are told that it takes around two days to cover the distance.

> *"Driven by the wind, the foamy necked ship then passed over the sea-waves most like a bird, until after the lapse of a normal space of time, <u>on the following day</u> the ring-prowed craft had reached the point where the travellers saw land, ocean cliffs standing out, steep headlands, broad*

sea-scarps; then the journey had concluded at the far end of the voyage."

The Beowulf Manuscript
RD Fulk Translation
Lines 216 – 224

Online Sailing Distance Calculator

The destination on the map above from the old Newhaven/ Seaford harbour entrance that leads directly to Hamsey is the island of Gotland. This journey by sail takes two days and six hours, as confirmed in the image above. (There was a large, navigable river through the centre of Denmark in the time of Beornwulf).

There are many reasons why, in my estimation, Gotland is the true location of the great hall, Heorot, and the most likely destination for Beowulf to be travelling to, so let us now begin to add some weight to this argument with the name "Gotland" itself, and see what it can tell us:

Gotland
Wikipedia

Etymology

Further information: Name of the Goths

The name of Gotland is closely related to that of the Geats and Goths.

As we can see here, the name, Gotland, is closely related to that of the Geats and the Goths. We have already established that Hrothgar holds many titles for various places related to the Geats and to Beowulf. There are further "Geat" references and other identifying names for the people of Beowulf within the text that I will now list below…

The Sea Geats

The Weder Geats

The Spear Danes

The Western Geats

The Eastern Geats

The Wind Loving Folk

So, here we have a definitive link to the existence of the Geats in Gotland, in the name of Gotland itself. Next in our list of names to examine is the title "Weder Geat", which has been repeatedly translated as "Weather Geat". There is, however, a far more noteworthy translation of this word, which comes in the form of "Season".

Weder (Old English)
WordSense Dictionary

Origin & history

From Proto-Germanic *wedrą, from Proto-Indo-European *wedʰrom. Cognate with Old Frisian weder (West Frisian waar), Old Saxon wedar (Low German Weder), Dutch weder, Old High German wetar (German Wetter), Old Norse veðr (Swedish väder, Danish vejr); and more distantly with Russian ведро.

Pronunciation

IPA: /ˈweder/

Noun

Weder (neut.)

Sky, weather, breeze, season.

As historical records have led us to believe that farming land was the main reason for the arrival of the Danes, this "seasonal" reference would make complete sense. It seems logical that the invading peoples from Gotland, Sweden, Norway, and Denmark would harvest the food they had produced in Britain during the summer and autumn months, with some returning home to their respective nations, carrying enough food to last the winter. It seems highly unlikely that any of these people would abandon their original settlements, never to return. More plausibly, you would expect them to return home and help to feed their own people. Thus, the title "Seasonal Geats" seems to be a more appropriate translation.

"Seafarers who ferried the gifts of the Geats here to our satisfaction used to say that he, brave in war, had the strength of thirty men in his hand-grip."

The Beowulf Manuscript
RD Fulk Translation
Line 374

Now, let us investigate the history of Gotland, regarding the era of Beornwulf, and see if we can provide any further information to support the theory for the great hall "Heorot" being located there.

The Mästermyr chest, an important artefact from the Viking Age, was found in Gotland.

On 16 July 1999, the world's largest Viking silver treasure, the Spillings Hoard, was found in a field at Spillings farm northwest of Slite. The silver treasure was divided into two parts weighing a total of 67 kg (148 lb) (27 kg (60 lb) and 40 kg (88 lb)) and consisted mostly of coins, about 14,000, from foreign countries, mostly Islamic. It also contained about 20 kg (44 lb) of bronze objects along with numerous everyday objects such as nails, glass beads, parts of tools, pottery, iron bands and clasps. The treasure was found by using a metal detector, and the finders fee, given to the farmer who owned the land, was over 2 million kronor (about US$308,000). The treasure was found almost by accident while filming a news report for TV4 about illegal treasure hunting on Gotland.

The number of Arab dirhams discovered on the island of Gotland alone is astoundingly high. In the various hoards located around the island, there are more of these silver coins than at any other site in Western Eurasia. The total sum is almost as great as the number that has been unearthed in the entire Muslim world. These coins moved north through trade between Rus merchants and the Abbasid Caliphate, along the Silver-Fur Road, and the money made by Scandinavian merchants would help northern Europe, especially Viking Scandinavia and the Carolingian Empire, as major commercial centers for the next several centuries.

This reference to the vast quantity of Arab Dirhams found on Gotland may infer a connection to the *Book of Judith*, found alongside the *Beowulf Manuscript*. It seems possible that the recorded attack in the Judith volume was on British shores and was perpetrated by the Vikings but with the additional help of Arab Nations. This is another incredibly complicated subject that requires too much time to include here but presents us with another fascinating possibility.

It is also critical to note that more late Anglo-Saxon coins have been found on Gotland than have ever been located in Britain. In relation to this, it seems highly probable that much of the silver paid to the Vikings to leave the shores of Britain, called "Danegeld", subsequently made its way over to Gotland. This would imply a strong link between the war leaders of the Vikings and their homeland, marking it out as a critical and noteworthy location during this period.

From this starting point, let us now look at the capital city of Gotland and see what we can discover regarding the Beornwulf/Viking era.

Visby in Gotland
Wikipedia

The name "Visby" comes from the Old Norse Vis (genetive singular of Vi), meaning "(pagan) place of sacrifices", and by, meaning "village". In the Gutasagan (mid-14th century), the place is referred to as just Wi, meaning "holy place, place of worship".

Visby is sometimes called "The City of Roses" or "The City of Ruins".

https://visitsweden.com/where-to-go/southern-sweden/gotland/

Visby's historic townscape features a high number of significant architectural buildings and structures dating back to the 13th century. Wrapping around the centuries-old centre, 'Ringmuren' (The Visby City Wall) – complete with towers and gates – was built between 1250 and 1288 and stretches across 3.5 kilometres.

For Viking enthusiasts, Gotland is something extra. The island is dotted with burial grounds from the Viking Era, such as a 15-hectare site in Stenkyrka with some 1,000 graves. The Gotland Museum's Fornsalen in Visby boasts Viking Age silver hoards,

and at Stavgard Vikingagard, a reconstructed Viking village, you can experience a day of the life of a Viking.

From this additional information, we can draw some important points in relation to the time of the Vikings and Beornwulf.

The first point is that the centre of Visby is called Ringmuren, in relation to the wall that surrounds it. This name bears a striking similarity to Ringmere, located in Sussex, where we discovered many etymological and geographical links to the *Beowulf Manuscript*. We should also remind ourselves here of the name, Ring Dane, for the people of Beowulf, which, it now seems may not refer solely to the practice of handing out golden arm rings by their lords but may also be linked to the names of the places that they lived in, Ringmuren and Ringmere. The geophysical markings left on the site beneath Malling Hill in Sussex would suggest that another enormous ring ditch and wall once stood there. It is easy to imagine how important a defensive structure of this sort would have been to all those who lived within them in such wild and dangerous times.

The next important point to consider is that Gotland is dotted with burial grounds from the Viking Era. This also fits well with the idea of an important, holy/historic location for the Danes in the time of Beowulf to both know about and want to go and visit/save. We also know that, whilst today, Gotland belongs to Sweden, it was originally, in the time of Beornwulf, a Danish-held country. We should also remember that executed Viking marauders were found on Malling Hill.

Returning to our proposed location for Heorot and the identity of Hrothgar, we should now look at the known kings of Gotland during the time that Beornwulf was alive.

King of the Goths
Wikipedia

This article is about the medieval title. For the migration-era Goths, see King of the Visigoths and King of the Ostrogoths.

The title of King of the Goths (Swedish: Götes konung; Danish: Goternes konge; Latin: gothorum rex) was for many centuries borne by both the kings of Sweden and the kings of Denmark.

In the Swedish case, the reference is to Götaland (land of the Geats), in the Danish case, to the island of Gotland (land of the Gutes).

Relevant list of Kings of Gotland from the era surrounding the life of Beornwulf

Sigfred: 770s–790s

Gudfred: 804–810, mentioned as Danish King in the Treaty of Heiligen 811. Alternate spellings: Godfred, Göttrick (German), Godric(Anglicized English), Gøtrik (Danish), Gudrød (Danish)

Hemming: 810–811/812 The Treaty of Heiligen was signed in 811 between the Danish King Hemming and Charlemagne.

Sigfred, nephew of Gudfred, and (Anlaufr), grandson or nephew of Harald, fought for the throne and both were killed, perhaps model for the legendary Sigurd Hring: c. 812

Harald Klak and his brothers Ragnfrid and Hemming Halfdansson: 812–813 and again from 819/827. From 826 *(The true year for the death of Beornwulf)*, he and his household lived in exile with the Frankish emperor Louis the Pious; he was baptised by the bishop of Mainz in Ingelheim am Rhein. The last references of Harald in the written sources are in the Annals of Fulda which records his execution for treason in 852.

In the historical references above, we have a list of three brothers who are kings of Denmark and are found to be ruling during the life of Beornwulf, 812-827. One of these kings is called Hemming Halfdansson. The *Beowulf Manuscript* tells us that Hrothgar has a father called Healfdene. These dates and names enable us to create a clear connection. Hemming is Halfdan's/son (The son of Halfdan), and Hrothgar is documented as having a father called Healfdene. It seems highly probable, therefore, that the historical Hemming (or one of his two brothers) is the true identity of Hrothgar from the *Beowulf Manuscript*. It is also very notable that the name Halfdan, or Healfdene, obviously derives from, "Half Dane". This would suggest a tie to a different nation in their lineage (Anglo-Saxon or Swedish) and would also mean that the king of the Danes, at this time, was not entirely Danish.

We are also informed in the historical record that early in his reign, Egberht (Ecgtheow) was forced to flee England to the court of the Frankish King, Charlemagne. We can speculate, therefore, that during this time, there is a possibility that Egberht (Ecgtheow) may have come into contact with Hemming, as recorded in the *Beowulf Manuscript*.

Hrothgar answered, helm of the Scyldings:
"I remember this man as the merest of striplings.
His father long dead now was Ecgtheow titled,
Him Hrethel the Geatman granted at home his
One only daughter; his battle-brave son."

Ecgberht and Charlemagne connection
Wikipedia

Ecgberht (770/775 – 839), also spelled Egbert, Ecgbert, Ecgbriht, Ecgbeorht, and Ecbert, was King of Wessex from 802 until his death in 839. His father was King Ealhmund of Kent. In the 780s, <u>Ecgberht was forced into exile to Charlemagne's court in the Frankish Empire by the kings Offa of Mercia and Beorhtric of Wessex</u>, but on Beorhtric's death in 802, Ecgberht returned and took the throne.

We can also create a strong connection between Hemming and Charlemagne during precisely the right time period.

Hemming and Charlemagne connection
Wikipedia

Hemming Halfdansson (died 837) was "of the Danish race, a most Christian leader". He was probably a son of Halfdan, a leading Dane who became a <u>vassal of Charlemagne</u> in 807. He was probably related to the Danish royal family, as "Hemming" was one of their favoured names.

It seems possible that sometime after the death of Beowulf, Gotland was conquered by the Swedish Vikings, which is why Hemming and his household lived in exile with the Frankish emperor Louis the Pious from the year 826 until his death. I suspect that the marauders found on Malling Hill were also from this period.

This chapter is not an exhaustive explanation of this subject. It has been extremely challenging to piece together the information I have deciphered so far in the form that it now takes, but perhaps someone can elaborate with further related details in the future. I do not doubt that these findings will be difficult for institutional historians to digest, but the copious amount of obvious connections here should speak clearly for themselves.

One final, astonishing connection remains concerning the great hall of Heorot, and this connection comes to us in the form of an old name for a village in East Sussex. The village name, "Hartfield", found at the edge of the Ashdown Forest (The Andreadeswold), derives directly from "Heorot", and this word has the same spelling that is used in the *Beowulf Manuscript*.

www.anchorhartfield.com
History of The Anchor Inn, Hartfield, East Sussex

The modern name of Hartfield derives from the Old English words "heorot" (hart and stag) and "feld" (pasture or open country). Today Hartfield is a quiet, leafy village, with a population of around two thousand, more famous for Winnie-the-Pooh than its industrial past.

www.picturesofengland.com/England/ East Sussex/Hartfield

The village grew out of a Saxon settlement, near the spot of one of the entrances to Sheffield Park, now owned by the National Trust.

Hartfield is also mentioned in Saxon Charters, but you will not be surprised to hear that Wikipedia has tied these references to a place called Harvel in North Kent. Strangely, no mention of an etymological link to Heorot is mentioned on the Wikipedia page for Hartfield, despite the stated connection to Heorot clearly mentioned in the reference for Harvel.

Harvel
Wikipedia

The village's name may derive from the names Halifield (Holy Field) or Heorot Field (Hartfield) mentioned in Saxon charters.

It is also noteworthy that Hartfield is adjacent to Holtye Village, which, given its proximity, is a further possibility for the location of "Ravensholt" within the Beowulf text. Additionally, Hartfield is a known ancient gateway into Sheffield Park. It has been suggested that one of the main etymological connections for "Geat" is "Gate". I now wonder if this is a factual representation. Borders and gateways can be controlled, and tolls can be imposed at these locations; King Alfred is known to have utilised the old Roman road network left behind in Britain, and Hartfield is on the major Roman artery of the London to Lewes Way, which we discussed previously. This would, therefore, be a sensible proposition for the location of a Saxon Hall. "Kingstanding" is also located nearby, which we referenced earlier in relation to the Battle of Ashdown.

Based on the evidence of this dense concentration of etymological connections, I would speculate that Hartfield was once Geatish-owned land (at least for a time) and that the name "Heorot" was also brought over to our shores from Gotland.

As a further consideration, it may be possible that the previously discussed "Council of Hertford" (relating to the formation of Clofesho) was held in Hartfield. The true name, on the original document states, "The Council of Herutford". Hartfield is famous for being the home of AA Milne who created Winnie the Pooh. It is also the famed location of Poohsticks Bridge, which crosses an ancient fording point along the river – (Heorot – Ford).

~ CHAPTER 16 ~

THE SEAFARER
THE WANDERER
AND THE RUIN

In a continuation of this research, I would now like to examine three, early Anglo-Saxon poems written by an unknown author. These poems are incredibly beautiful; they speak of the sea voyages of the era, the unknown ruins that (I believe) the Romans had left behind, and the sadness of a wanderer who is seeking a new home in distant lands. The emotive language presents us with a more realistic view of the harsher realities of the time and are, in my opinion, early masterpieces of literature.

For our purposes, while reading these poems, please picture a journey from Sussex to Gotland regarding the first two sections of the poems, and then consider The Ruin to be a description of the Ouse Valley once the wanderer has returned home. I will include a small, noteworthy snippet from each poem below, but I would highly recommend reading them all in full if you would like to experience a taste of the genuine emotions of an amazing man from a distant past...

These poems are speculatively dated to the eighth or ninth century and were published in the 10th century in The Exeter Book.

~ The Seafarer ~

Let me speak, in truth, of my life,
tell of toilsome days of travel,
days suffering hardship,
bitterness of heart:
how I endured sorrowful times on ships,
on dreadful rolling seas.
Hard night's watch at the ship's prow
was by frequent task,
the ship often tossed along towering cliffs,
afflicted with cold feet, numbed by frost, chill bonds.
My sorrows burned in my heart,
I sighed forth hunger that rent my mind,
I, the sea-weary man.

He who fares so prosperously on land
knows not that I have spent great careworn winters
an exile on the ice-cold sea,
cut off from kin,
hung round with icicles,
hail pelting me in showers,
I heard nothing but the booming sea
and the cold billowing sea-waves.
Sometimes I heard the song of the swan,
seized gladness in the cry of the gannet

and the sound of the curlew, instead of
the laughter of men; in the screaming gull,
instead of the clanking mead-cups.

On the sea, storms beat against the rocky cliffs,
the icy-feathered tern echoed the storm-winds,
as, too, the wing-soaked eagle.
No protector could comfort the heart in need.
He who holds the bliss of life, proud-flushed with wine,
who suffers few hardships in cities, disbelieves
how often in weariness I had to dwell upon the ocean path.
The shadow of night grew dark,
snow flew in from the north,
fast bound the land,
hail, coldest of grains, falling upon the earth.

~ The Wanderer ~

Wretched, I tie my heart with ropes
Far from my home, far from my kinsmen
Since a hole in the ground hid my chief
Long ago. Laden with cares,
Weary, I crossed the confine of waves,
Sought the troop of a dispenser of treasure,
Far or near to find the man
Who knew my merits in the mead hall,
Who would foster a friendless man,
Treat me to joys. He who has put it to a test
Knows how cruel a companion is sorrow
For one who has few friendly protectors.
Exile guards him, not wrought gold,
A freezing heart, not the fullness of the earth.

He remembers warriors, the hall, rewards,
How, as a youth, his friend honoured him at feasts,
The gold-giving prince. Joy has perished,

~ The Ruin ~

Wondrous is this foundation — the fates have broken
and shattered this city; the work of giants crumbles.
The roofs are ruined, the towers toppled,
frost in the mortar has broken the gate,
torn and worn and shorn by the storm,
eaten through with age. The earth's grasp
holds the builders, rotten, forgotten,
the hard grip of the ground, until a hundred
generations of men are gone. This wall, rust-stained
and moss-covered, has endured one kingdom after another,
stood in the storm, steep and tall, then tumbled.
The foundation remains, felled by the weather,
it fell.....
grimly ground up....
......cleverly created....
...... a crust of mud surrounded...
..... put together a swift
and subtle system of rings; one of great wisdom
wondrously bound the braces together with wires.
Bright were the buildings, with many bathhouses,
noble gables and a great noise of armies,
many a mead hall filled with men's joys,
until mighty fate made an end to all that.
The slain fell on all sides, plague-days came,
and death destroyed all the brave swordsmen;
the seats of their idols became empty wasteland,
the city crumbled, its re-builders collapsed

beside their shrines. So now these courts are empty,
and the rich vaults of the vermilion roofs
shed their tiles. The ruins toppled to the ground,
broken into rubble, where once many a man
glad-minded, gold-bright, bedecked in splendour,
proud, full of wine, shone in his war-gear,
gazed on treasure, on silver, on sparking gems,
on wealth, on possessions, on the precious stone,
on the bright capital of a broad kingdom.
Stone buildings stood, the wide-flowing stream
threw off its heat; a wall held it all
in its bright bosom where the baths were,
hot in its core, a great convenience.
They let them gush forth.....
the hot streams over the great stones,
under....
until the circular pool .... hot...
.....where the baths were.

I would be interested to know if, after reading these three portions of the poems, you can see any similarities to the subject matter we have examined throughout this investigation.

It seems that if anyone could write these poems with such stunning parallels to the *Beowulf* text, it would be the man himself, Beornwulf. Notably, given everything we have discovered, the last poem sample (*The Ruin*) appears to be a literal, precise description of the same treasure vault that appears in *Beowulf*. We can be fairly certain of this, as the same language is used for precise and obscure details. Let's look at the description of the treasure leavers and of the treasure vault in *Beowulf* once more, and then the section of the poem, *The Ruin*, one more time to confirm the links.

"There was in that house of earth many of such golden treasures, as someone, I know not who, among men in days of yore had there prudently concealed, jewels of price and mighty heirlooms of a noble race. All of them death had taken in times before, and now he too alone of the proven warriors of his people, who longest walked the earth, watching, grieving for his friends, hoped but for the same fate, that he might only a little space enjoy those long-hoarded things. _A barrow already waited upon the earth nigh to the watery waves, new-made upon a headland, secured by binding spells._ Therein did the keeper lade a portion right worthy to be treasured of the wealth of noble men, of plated gold; and a few words he spake. 'Keep thou now, earth, what mighty men could not, the wealth of warriors. Lo! Aforetime in thee it was that good men found it! Death in battle, cruel and deadly evil, hath taken each mortal man of my people, who have forsaken this life, the mirth of warriors in the hall. I have none that may bear sword, or burnish plated cup and precious drinking vessel. _The proud host hath vanished away._ Now shall the hard helm, gold-adorned, be stripped of its plates; those who should burnish it, who should polish its visor for battle are asleep, and the armour too that stood well the bite of iron swords in war amid bursting shields now followeth its wearer to decay. The ringed corslet no more may widely fare in company of a prince of war, upon the side of mighty men. There is no glad sound of harp, no mirth of instrument of music, nor doth good hawk sweep through the hall, nor the swift horse tramp the castle-court. _Ruinous death hath banished hence many a one of living men._"

The Beowulf Manuscript
JRR Tolkien Translation
Lines 1,876 -1,888

"Then I have heard that speedily the son of Wihstan, when these words were spoken, did hearken to his wounded lord in combat stricken, striding in his netlike mail, his corslet for battle woven, under the barrow's vault. Then, passing by _the seat_, that young knight proudhearted, filled with the joy of victory, beheld a host of hoarded jewels, gold glistening that lay upon the ground, marvellous things upon the wall, the very lair of that old serpent in the dim light flying, and ewers standing there, vessels of men of bygone days, reft of those who cared for them, their fair adornment crumbling. There was many a helm old and rusted, a multitude of twisted armlets in strange devices twined. Treasure, gold hidden in the earth, easily may overtake the heart of any of the race of men – let him beware who will! There too he saw a banner hanging all wrought of gold, high above the hoard, the chiefest of all marvellous things of handicraft, woven by skill of fingers. Therefrom a radiance issued, that he might plain perceive that space beneath the earth, and all the precious things survey. Of the serpent there was nought to see; nay, the sword had taken him. Then, as I have heard, within that mound the Hoard and _ancient work of giants_ did one man plunder, lading his bosom with dish and goblet at his own sweet will; the banner too, he seized, of standards the most shining-fair."

The Beowulf Manuscript
JRR Tolkien Translation
Lines 2,309 – 2,331

"Hard by the rock-face that hale veteran, a good man who had gone repeatedly into combat and danger and come through, saw a _stone arch and a gushing stream that burst from the barrow, blazing and wafting a deadly heat_."

The Beowulf Manuscript
Seamus Heaney Translation
Lines 2,542-2,549

~ The Ruin ~

Wondrous is this foundation — the fates have broken
and shattered this city; <u>the work of giants</u> crumbles.
The roofs are ruined, the towers toppled,
frost in the mortar has broken the gate,
torn and worn and shorn by the storm,
eaten through with age. The earth's grasp
holds the builders, rotten, forgotten,
the hard grip of the ground, until a hundred
generations of men are gone. <u>This wall, rust-stained</u>
<u>and moss-covered, has endured one kingdom after another,</u>
stood in the storm, <u>steep and tall, then tumbled.</u>
<u>The foundation remains</u>, felled by the weather,
it fell…..
grimly ground up….
……<u>cleverly created</u>….
…… <u>a crust of mud surrounded</u>….
….. put together a swift
and subtle system of rings; one of great wisdom
wondrously <u>bound the braces together with wires</u>.
Bright were the buildings, <u>with many bathhouses</u>,
noble gables and a great noise of armies,
many a mead hall filled with men's joys,
until mighty fate made an end to all that.
The slain fell on all sides, <u>plague-days came,</u>
<u>and death destroyed all the brave swordsmen;</u>
the <u>seats</u> of their idols became empty wasteland,
the city crumbled, its re-builders collapsed
beside their shrines. So now these courts are empty,
and the rich vaults of the vermilion roofs
shed their tiles. The ruins toppled to the ground,
broken into rubble, where once many a men

glad-minded, gold-bright, bedecked in splendour,
proud, full of wine, shone in his war-gear,
gazed on treasure, on silver, on sparking gems,
on wealth, on possessions, on the precious stone,
<u>on the bright capital of a broad kingdom.</u>
Stone buildings stood, <u>the wide-flowing stream</u>
<u>threw off its heat; a wall held it all</u>
<u>in its bright bosom where the baths were,</u>
hot in its core, a great convenience.
They let them gush forth....
the hot streams over the great stones,
under...
<u>until the circular pool .... hot...</u>
<u>....where the baths were.</u>

"*Against his will, he went to where he knew a solitary hall of earth, a vault under ground, <u>nigh to the surges of the deep and warring waves</u>. All filled within was it with cunning work and golden wire. The monstrous guardian eager and ready in battle ancient beneath the earth kept those golden treasures – no easy bargain that for any among men to win.*"

The Beowulf Manuscript
JRR Tolkien Translation
Lines 2,024 – 2,030

It seems worthwhile here to note the reference in this poem to the many bathhouses of the area in which it is set. We have already learned of some evidence for bathhouses in the reality of the Roman geography/archaeology in the Ouse Valley. (I believe there are many more, waiting to be found) It is also worth an additional recollection of the Mons Badonicus etymological reference in relation to the Arthurian era (Badon meaning "to bathe") and then to recall that Beddingham sits directly beneath Mt Caburn, where a Roman bathhouse was discovered and excavated in the 1980s.

As an interesting side note, Virginia Woolf lived in Beddingham at a place called Asham or Asheham House. Sadly, she did not own the property and was forced to leave. This house was then left to go to ruin and was subsequently demolished; the site was then turned into a cement works. This cement works eventually became a landfill site. I will leave it to you to look into the awful poison that has been buried there since it took on this purpose and also where the "overflow" and seepage from it has made its way to. It beggars belief that this was allowed to happen in an area that was a known Saxon minster, and the home of such a noted author. While living at Aseham house, Woolf wrote a beautiful short story about the property titled *A Haunted House*.

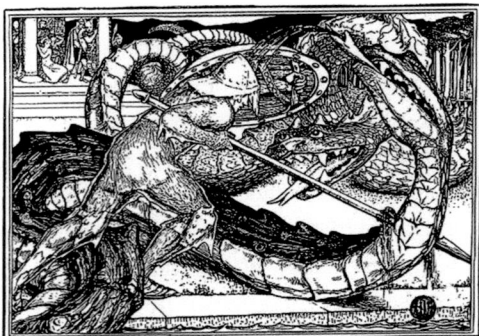

RAGNAR DOES BATTLE WITH THE SERPENTS

~ CHAPTER 17 ~

RAGNAR LODBROK

Semi-legendary kings
Wikipedia

Ragnar Lodbrok, a legendary king probably in the 9th century, only appears in sagas and late histories, and these accounts are wildly inconsistent. He may be a composite character, a chimera of several historical kings and vikings.

There is one further, seemingly improbable connection to Beowulf for us to consider. This comes in the form of Ragnar Lodbrok, a legendary figure from the viking era. His story has been preserved for us in *The Saga of Ragnar Lodbrok*, which is included in an ancient text named *The Volsunga Saga*. The recent TV series, *Vikings*, also follows a fairly close resemblance to the documented history of the legendary warrior king and his infamous sons: Ivar Boneless, Ubba Ragnarson, Bjorn Ironside, Vitsek Ragnarson and Sigurd Snake in the Eye. The curious links to the *Beowulf* legend come to us thanks to some unlikely but noteworthy parallels regarding Beowulf and Ragnar's names, their descriptions, and most notably, the time they were alive and the circumstances of their deaths.

First of all, the name Lodbrok is said to be related to the hairy, bear fur trousers he wore. Lod means hairy, and brok is from brooks, the old English word for trousers. "Ragnar Hairy Trousers" is a fairly uninspiring but accurate translation.

The reason that this reference may loosely link to Beowulf himself is that the name Beorn translates directly to "Bear" (Bear-Wolf). Ragnar is thought to have been a very large, fierce warrior who wore bear fur trousers, so this presents us with a slight descriptive parallel to Beowulf.

The most important factor to consider when attempting to link these two characters together is found in the time and the nature of how they died. Both Ragnar and Beowulf are, according to their respective stories, killed by serpents. Additionally, if we now consider that Beornwulf was indeed Beowulf, we can bring King Ecgberht back into the equation. Historically, with regard to the Ragnar Lodbrok legend, we are led to believe that somewhere in England, King Ecgberht captures Ragnar and hands him over to Aella of Mercia, who then decides to execute him. Aella throws Ragnar into a pit of serpents, where he is bitten by them and killed by their poison. Beowulf is the son of King Ecgtheow and also meets his end when bitten by a poisonous serpent. It is worthwhile noting that the modern-day translation of the word "serpents" in the *Saga of Ragnar Lodbrok* has now been transformed into the image of a pit of snakes, of which there are very few in Britain, and only the Adder is venomous. However, we only need one serpent in the form of the dragon to posit a plausible misinterpretation and subsequent elaboration to the "Chinese whispered" story.

A further notable detail is that both Beowulf and Ragnar, in their respective stories, take defensive measures against the bite of the serpent. Ragnar tars his trousers so that the fangs cannot penetrate them in preparation for an earlier encounter with a different dragon. Beowulf forges a shield made of iron to protect him from the heat of the flames. The seemingly improbable chance of finding two separate characters with these descriptive parallels reflected in the timing and nature of their deaths, preserved in Anglo-Saxon and Scandinavian stories (of which there are incredibly few – less than around ten), seems extraordinarily low. If we then add the Ecgberht – Beornwulf and Ecgberht – Ragnar connection, it becomes even more unlikely that these events are unrelated. Is it possible that Ragnar and Beowulf are really the same person, recorded with different names? It seems probable that, once again, the countries in which the respective stories were written had different titles for these same individuals.

A last thought to consider regarding the Beowulf/Ragnar connection comes to us in a reference that we covered briefly in chapter eight. It is from the old map of Lewes and Ringmere. Here, we find the name of a settlement called Hauleland. This old fortified burgh is now known as Halland. Halland is the current name for a town in Kattegat on the Swedish coast, which, from his story, we have been led to believe was one of Ragnar's original homes. Directly beneath Halland (in Sussex) is the battle site of Terrible Down, which may also create a further connection to King Alfred during the invasion of the Great Heathen Army.

These observances are purely speculations to consider, and by no means do I pretend to know the absolute truth of this matter. It is nigh on impossible to do so with the information we have available. Each of these tales is also the recorded version of a story from the individual who wrote or composed them, which leaves us with a very blurred picture of the actual truth. Failing the invention of a time machine, drawing surmounting parallels that reflect a genuine connection in a noteworthy manner appears to be the best that anyone will ever be able to do, and these notable correlations seem too complimentary to ignore.

~ CHAPTER 18 ~

KINGSTON, DENTON, BEDDINGHAM AND MEDELHAMESTEDE

This chapter has been included to provide some highly relevant, supporting information regarding the historical importance of the areas surrounding Lewes and Hamsey.

We will begin with the fairly obvious etymology of Kingston, which is a village situated above the head of Lewes that sits beneath one of the largest and steepest hills on the South Downs called Castle Hill, which gives us a good clue for what once may have stood there.

Kingston Etymology
Wikipedia

In the case of settlements outside England, from King's

+ -ton ("town"), in reference to monarchs of the British Empire. In the case of settlements within England, a development from earlier Old English Cinges tūn or Cynges tūn ("king's town or manor"), in reference to various monarchs.

***

It would now be worthwhile to know that:

1. King Aethelwulf is currently thought to have been buried in Steyning in West Sussex.

2. The capital of Britain up to the time of William the Conqueror (1066). was Winchester in West Sussex, not London.

3. King Aethelstan, in the year 925, was crowned King in "Kingston" (the same year as his witan at Hamsey/ Hammes).

The original *Anglo-Saxon Chronicle* entry for Aethelstan's coronation reads "Cyningeston", which translates directly to "Kingston". It does not include the suffix "on Thames". Additionally, I have always felt it would be quite unlikely for an early King of Wessex, whose capital was in Winchester, to decide to be crowned in London. This is not to say that London was not an important location during the life of Aethelstan, but it is a known fact that it was not the capital of Britain at this time, so why would he decide to be crowned there? Additionally, I have not been able to locate any supporting information to state that the coronation definitively took place in London.

There is an ancient church at the foot of Castle Hill in Kingston by Lewes called the Church of St Pancras. Perhaps, and this is purely speculative, this modest place of worship, more reflective of his period and located much closer to the capital of his kingdom, would be a more likely location for the ceremony. With all of the royal ancestral ties we have now covered in relation to Sussex, Lewes, Hamsey, Ringmer, and Malling, it would appear that this is a likely reality. We can also place Aethelstan in this precise area of Sussex in the year 925, as we have already discovered that he held a witan at Hamsey Church in exactly the same year. You can walk from Hamsey to Kingston nr Lewes in under an hour. We have also been informed that Aethelstan had two royal mints in Lewes, marking it out as an important location during his life. I will not go too deeply into a further subject regarding "The Old Minster" (Clofesho), but I am sure you can understand the inference if you are inclined toward any research of your own.

Hughes, J D (1986) King Athelstan's 'witan', the charter evidence, Durham theses, Durham University.

**Available at Durham E-Theses Online:
http://etheses.dur.ac.uk/7038/**

THE MEETING PLACES OF THE KING'S "WITAN", 928-34

It is evident from the map and the above list that the meeting places of the "Witan" were concentrated in Wessex, the heartland of the Wessex Saxon dynasty to which Aethelstan belonged.

Concerning the ancestral ties of the early Anglo-Saxon royal family in these Southern lands, I would also like to add some further details relating to the location of the tombstone of King Aethelwulf, which we find today propped up in the porch of a church called St Cuthbert's, in a town named

Steyning. His bones have now been transferred to Winchester, but it is important to note that Winchester was certainly not where he was originally buried and, very likely, not even where he lived. If we look at the map below, we can see that Steyning is located right next to another town called Bramber, and it is here that we find the isolated ruins of what must once have been a rather spectacular castle.

In relation to this, hidden away in the details available to us on another ancient church located in the castle grounds of Bramber called The Church of St Nicholas, we find some pertinent information regarding the burials that were once located there. Below, we are provided with some important clues from an interesting story regarding an early land dispute between William de Braose of Bramber (a Templar Knight) and some monks of the nearby church in Steyning.

William de Braose, First Lord of Bramber
Land disputes
Wikipedia

Braose built a bridge at Bramber and demanded tolls

from ships travelling further along the river to the busy port at Steyning. The monks challenged this, and they also disputed Braose's right to bury people in the churchyard of his new church of Saint Nicholas at Bramber, demanding the burial fees for themselves, despite the church having been built to serve the castle and not the town. The monks then produced forged documents to defend their position and were unhappy with the failure of their claim on Hastings, which was very similar. They claimed the same freedoms and land tenure in Hastings as King Edward had given them at Steyning. On a technicality, King William was bound to uphold all rights and freedoms held by the abbey before King Edward's death, but the monks had already been expelled ten years before that. William wanted to hold Hastings for himself for strategic reasons, and he ignored the problem until 1085, when he confirmed the abbey's claims to Steyning but compensated it for its claims at Hastings with land in the manor of Bury, near Pulborough in Sussex. In 1086 King William called his sons, barons and bishops to court (the last time an English king presided personally, with his full court, to decide a matter of law) to settle the Steyning disputes, which took a full day. The result was that the abbey won over William de Braose, forcing him to curtail his bridge tolls, to give up various encroachments onto the abbey's lands, including a farmed rabbit warren, a park, 18 burgage tenements, a causeway, and a channel used to fill his moat. Braose also had to organise a mass exhumation of all Bramber's dead, the bodies being transferred to the abbey's churchyard of Saint Cuthman's in Steyning.

So, as we can see, around the year 1086, all of Bramber's dead were transferred to the abbey's churchyard of Saint Cuthman's in Steyning, where we now find King Aethelwulf's tombstone, not in the graveyard, but in the front porch. This seems like a highly probable reason for how it ended up there. Bramber was clearly another important location, situated between Lewes and Winchester.

It appears that this site must also have meant something personally to King Aethelwulf for him to have chosen to be buried there. This is vital information to consider when attempting to locate the true home of Aethelwulf and the people connected to him.

The next two sites to bring to your attention (one of which we have already discussed) are called Denton and Beddingham. These names are discussed in a surviving Anglo-Saxon charter, and both of these villages are located on the old shoreline of the Ouse Valley. As mentioned, Beddingham sits beneath Mount Caburn, and Denton is a little further back towards the coast on the old tidal estuary.

Below is a portion of a charter written in the year 801. This charter is a valuable document with regard to placing some of the known locations for the kings and bishops of the time directly into the Ouse Valley.

Sussex Anglo-Saxon Charters

In the year of our Lord's incarnation 801, the fifth year of Coenwulf, king of the Mercians, there arose a certain disagreement between Coenwulf and Withun, bishop of the South Saxons, concerning land of the aforesaid bishop, that is, 25 (hides) in Denton. The king said that it ought more properly belong to the monastery in

Beddingham; the bishop said that it had been given to his predecessors in the church which is in Selsey. The king had it in mind to deprive him of a portion of his heritage, if Withun, bishop of the aforesaid province, had not convinced him with testimony and canonical phrases, and mitigated the pernicious idea of the king's majesty, and with humble supplication asked that in innocence he should not be deprived of the Church's heritage. Then the king pronounced his legal decision, agreeing with the bishop and granting that he should be restored to his own by a charter, and that with his successors it should remain there without any trouble. And this he ordered to be put into writing in the presence of the whole synod at Chelsea, so that none of his successors should molest him or interfere with the church in any way, witnessed by those whose names appear written below. I Coenwulf, king of the Mercians, have agreed and signed this.

———————————————————

Here, we have been given two names for locations within the land of the South Saxons. The first is Denton, and the second is Beddingham. We are told here that these sites are being governed by King Coenwulf, who we have already discovered was the king that preceded Beornwulf. So let us now have a look at where these two locations are in relation to Lewes, Hamsey, Ringmer and the Ouse Valley:

In the translation we are provided with from the charter above, we are also told: "And this he ordered to be put into writing in the presence of the whole synod at Chelsea." Here, we have a further example of a translator making an assumption based on the information he has available. The reality here is that the word for Chelsea, in the original document, reads "Celchide", which translates to "the chalk landing place", of which there are many along the Ouse Valley and all along the shores of coastal Britain. I believe that this name is in reference to either the cliffs of Cliffe High Street at the foot of Lewes or the vast chalk pit below Offham Hill that would once have been home to a sizeable harbour located directly below it. The last significant addition to the town of Lewes was a housing estate called Landport (a good clue), which is now located here. There is also what appears to be a small settlement or burial ground here, just below the peak of Offham Hill with a direct view across the valley to Malling Hill. Between these two peaks sits the promontory of Hammes and Old St Peter's church.

It now seems pertinent to note that there appears to be a peculiar bias from past historians who have confidently placed many notable events from this early Anglo-Saxon era, either in or around London. This seems to be an error that modern historians have not yet recognised. In relation to this, it is necessary to reiterate a few critical points. The capital of Britain, up to the time of William the Conqueror, was Winchester in Wessex; it was not London. Nearly all kings from the preceding era were located in Wessex, Sussex, and

Kent, not London. King Aethelwuf's tombstone, which is found in Steyning to this very day, actually places him there beyond all doubt, not in London. King Aethelstan's coronation is recorded as occurring in Kingston and not in "Kingston (by the Thames)". The evidence for placing his coronation there is also non-existent.

I have pondered this strange problem of "London bias" for many years, and it appears probable that historians of their day, perhaps considering London to have always been the most important location in England, placed these witans there purely out of a misinterpreted bias. With little examination of these notable errors up to the present day, modern historians have simply been reiterating old fallacies that have now stuck fast. A fantastic thesis written by Angela Marion Smith, published in 2014, examines the extensive documentary evidence that, unusually, Aethelstan had *two* coronation ceremonies, which also does not appear to be widely known at this time. Perhaps one of these was indeed in London, but I would hazard an educated guess that the recorded coronation in the *Anglo-Saxon Chronicle*, was in Kingston by Lewes.

Two further charters are also relevant to our investigation. In the first, we continue with the matter of the land dispute discussed at Denton, but in this charter, we are also led straight back to Beornwulf and, quite possibly, a new, combined name for Clofesho and Hammes, of which you should now be very familiar.

Sussex Anglo-Saxon Charters

In the name of the Lord! In the year 825, from the incarnation of Christ, the third of the indiction, the second year of the reign of Beornwulf king of the

Mercians, there was a synod at Clobesham, under the chairmanship of Archbishop Wulfred; for after the death of Coenwulf, king of the Mercians, there had arisen many quarrels and disagreements between various kings, nobles, and bishops and ministers of the church of God, on various matters of secular business; so that in various places the churches of God were much despoiled of goods, of lands, of tribute, and of all manner of things. Among them Coenred, bishop of the South Saxons, had been robbed of a certain part of the land at that church, 25 (hides) which are called Denton; Plegheard the abbot had formerly given it with his own body to the episcopal see which is in Selsey; before that; King Offa had granted it to him in writing from the inheritance of the church at Beddingham, which he himself had acquired as his own heritage. Then in the aforesaid synod it was decreed that the bishop, with the unanimous agreement and advice of the bishops, abbots, and nobles, should lawfully receive the inheritance of the church without any interference, just as before it was decreed between King Coenwulf and Withun about the possession of the same land, at *Chelsea *"Celchide"* in the presence of archbishop Aethelheard, in the third year of King Coenwulf. And this was performed in the presence of the whole synod at Clobesham, with the agreement and permission of the king and the nobles and archbishops, whose names are given below, and who confirmed by making the mark of the cross of Christ. I, Wulfred, archbishop, sign and confirm this declaration, for greater security, with the sign of the Saviour. Aethelwalh, bishop. Ceolberht, bishop. Wihtred aboot. Sigered, alderman. Eadwulf, aldermen. Eadberht, alderman. Ealhstan. Ealdred.

Eadbald. If anyone, moreover, (God forbid!) attempts to infringe this grant, let him know that he will be cursed and barred from all religious society, unless he shall first have made amends to the satisfaction of God and man.

This charter is useful in a number of ways. Firstly, we are provided with a connection between Beornwulf and Clobesham. This name appears to be a combination of the words Clovesho and Ham. Now that we are aware of all the links we have already covered regarding Beornwulf's presence at Clovesho, Hammes and Beowulf, it seems very likely that, once again, Old St Peter's church at Hamsey is the location of this synod at Clobesham.

Next, we have a reference that Offa, an infamous King of the Mercians in the 700s, not only held land at Beddingham in the century prior to Beornwulf but also, we can see that this land is described as "his own heritage". This brings a further, solid connection between the early Anglo-Saxon Kings and their presence in the lands of the Ouse Valley. Curiously, our modern historical sources suggest that the village of Offham by Lewes on the outskirts of Hamsey has no connection to Offa, but two different Offham Villages in Sussex and Kent do directly connect to Offa. It is known that the Offham by Lewes has had multiple name changes throughout the years. I am, however, highly inclined toward believing that Offa is indeed connected to Offham by Lewes, from the simple fact that we have an original surviving charter stating he owned land that was his heritage, just a few hundred yards downriver from Offham, at Beddingham. Perhaps, as has occurred with Gote Lane, Offham was originally named Offham, then went through some changes until it arrived back at Offham again in the modern day.

It is also worthwhile noting that this charter provides us with a list of lords that are closely connected to Beornwulf, the ruling king at the witan. Noticeably, we have a similar pattern presenting itself here, with the suffix to all of the names matching with the characters we covered in the earlier chapter, The Characters Within Beowulf and the Early Anglo-Saxon Kings. The prefix in this instance is Ead or Eal. If we remove this prefix, we are once again left with wulf, bert, stan, red, and bald, who are all aldermen. I suspect that in this instance, the Ead or Eal relates to Alderman as Aethel does to The Noble. All of these titles are relevant to these individuals, so we could infer that they are very likely, once again, the same people.

We should now move on to another well-documented location within the *Anglo-Saxon Chronicle*. This site is recorded within many existing charters and has various iterations of its name:

The name "Medeshamstede"
Wikipedia

Medeshamstede, as it appears in a 12th-century manuscript from Peterborough Abbey, copying a purportedly 7th-century charter.

The name has been interpreted by a placename authority as "homestead belonging to Mede".

An alternative description is 'Medu' meaning Mead then 'Hamme' a village on a river and 'Steð' (the ð is pronounced th) meaning a bank or sea shore (the sea was about 4.5 metres higher in early Saxon times), so the 'Mead village in the valley with a landing stage'

According to the Peterborough version of the *Anglo-*

Saxon Chronicle, written in the 12th century, this name was given at the time of the foundation of a monastery there in the 7th century, owing to the presence of a spring called "Medeswæl", meaning "Medes-well". However the name is commonly held to mean "homestead in the meadows", or similar, on an assumption that "Medes-" means "meadows".

The earliest reliable occurrence of the name is in Bede's Ecclesiastical History, where it is mentioned in the genitive Latinised form "Medeshamstedi", in a context dateable prior to the mid-670s. However the area had long been inhabited, for example at Flag Fen, a Bronze Age settlement a little to the east, and at the Roman town of Durobrivae, on the other side of the River Nene, and some five miles to the west. It is possible that "Medeshamstede" began as the name of an unrecorded, pre-existing Anglian settlement, at or near the site.

Another early form of this name is "Medyhæmstede", in an 8th-century Anglo-Saxon royal charter preserved at Rochester Cathedral. Also found is "Medelhamstede", in the late 10th century Ælfric of Eynsham's account of the life of St Æthelwold of Winchester, and on a contemporary coin of King Æthelred II, where it is abbreviated to "MEÐEL." A much later development is the form "Medeshampstede", *(a different place altogether)* and similar variants, which presumably arose alongside similar changes, e.g. from Old English "[North] Hamtun" to the modern "Northampton". Despite the fact that they are, therefore, strictly unhistorical, forms such as "Medeshampstede" are found in later historical writings.

Locally, Anglo-Saxon records use "Medeshamstede"

up to about the reign of King Æthelred II, but modern historians generally use it only to the reign of his father King Edgar, and use "Peterborough Abbey" for the monastery thereafter, until it changes to "Peterborough Cathedral" in the reign of King Henry VIII.

As we have already connected Old St Peters church at the foot of Lewes to Hammes and Clofesho, let us now revisit a location within the modern-day village of Ringmer, right next to Gote Lane. This location is called Middleham.

"Ham" names surrounding Ringmer

Hamsey

Ham Lane

Stoneham Farm

Chalkham Farm

Offham

Beddingham

Middleham

Wellingham (The Well in Ham)
(*'Medeswael' referenced above)

If we now recall that Hamsey was the location of an old port and that the vast river network upstream from here was called the Midwinde, and additionally, that all of those rivers fed back to this one location, we can begin to understand why it was once so important and was also so well documented. This heavy concentration of ham names, coupled with the

Middleham and Middlewinder river references, along with other names in the area, such as "Saxon Down" and "Saxon Cross", all confirm for us that this is a highly probable site for Medeshamestede.

A curious and possibly connected side note is that the etymology of Beddingham is "Beadyngham" – "Beada's Ham" – "Baeda" – The Venerable Bede? To add a little support to this etymological theory, there was once a Roman villa, a bathhouse, and then a monastery located there. In addition, it was once important enough to have been discussed and recorded in the *Anglo-Saxon Chronicle* in the year 801 and was a known Saxon royal minster that passed from Cedwalla to Offa to Alfred, then to Earl Godwin and finally, to Harold Godwinson. I now wonder if Bede was connected to this monastery somehow.

Beddingham Reference
Wikipedia

Beddingham was a Saxon royal minster. It was probably seized by Offa of Mercia after his annexation of Sussex early in the 770s. One of Offa's coins was found there. Once back in Saxon possession, the land was <u>bequeathed by King Alfred</u> to his nephew Aethelhelm, and the manor <u>later held by Earl Godwin</u>.

This reference is notable for bringing further significant ties to Lewes and the old Anglo-Saxon royal family. Earl Godwin is the father of Harold Godwinson, the last Anglo-Saxon king who fought against William the Conqueror at the Battle of Hastings. I have already mentioned that on a site called St John's Sub Castro, there was once a proposed Roman encampment. This site sits on a small bluff above the Pells Swimming Pool. This swimming pool, as previously discussed, is fed by two cold-water natural springs to this very day. It would make a lot of sense to build an encampment here if we are to consider an army's need for washing and clean water. What is not so well known or associated is that in the far reaches of the burial grounds of the church, there once stood an ancient prison site. Today, set into the walls of St John's sub-Castro church, a tombstone purported to be from this old prison site now makes up a portion of the masonry. The inscription reads:

> HERE IS ENCLOSED A KNIGHT OF THE
> ROYAL FAMILY OF DENMARK WHOSE NAME,
> MAGNUS, INDICATES HIS ROYAL LINEAGE.
> RELINQUISHING HIS GREATNESS, HE
> ASSUMES THE DEPORTMENT OF A LAMB AND
> EXCHANGES FOR A LIFE OF AMBITION, THAT
> OF A LOWLY ANCHORITE.

The interesting, related link here is that a certain Magnus was a known son of Harold Godwinson. It has also been noted that "the emphasis on a Danish Lineage would suggest a pre-conquest dating for the memorial". I would hazard a guess that the memorial actually dates to within 30 or 40 years *after* the Norman conquest.

Magnus Godwinson
Wikipedia

Magnus (1068) was a son of Harold Godwinson, King of England. He was, in all likelihood, driven into exile in Dublin by the Norman conquest of England, along with two of his brothers, and from there took part in one, or perhaps two, expeditions to south-western England, but with little military success. They probably cost him his life.

It seems unlikely that there were multiple Magnus characters of royal Danish lineages that were important enough to have their name and tombstone set into the wall of a church sometime around the Norman conquest. If we now consider that Offa, Earl Godwin, and then Harold Godwinson all held titles for the Royal Saxon Minster at Beddingham, directly across the river Ouse from Lewes, and then we include the proximity of Lewes to Hastings, and then add this memorial written in stone into the equation, alongside all of the information we have already discovered on Clofesho, Beornwulf, and Ringmere by Hammes, we can begin to see the true importance of this area within the county of Sussex with fresh eyes. It seems highly likely that Lewes and the surrounding areas were critical historical locations for the kings of the pre-conquest era. Only once William had taken the country does it appear that the town's significance slowly faded from memory and London became the new centre of Britain. This is not to say that royal ties to the town of Lewes died completely at this time. Three centuries after Hastings, another battle took place in Lewes with King Henry III and his son Edward Longshanks, fighting against Simon De Montford and his Barons. King Henry and Edward were defeated here, and it would seem that Lewes castle was partially razed at this time.

HERE STOOD SNELLINGS MILL, IN WHICH RICHARD, KING OF THE ROMANS AND BROTHER OF HENRY III, SOUGHT REFUGE DURING THE BATTLE OF LEWES IN 1264. "RICHARD, THAH THOU BE EVER TRICHARD, TRICHEN SHALT THOU NEVERMORE"

Sign from the top of Lewes High Street, near to St Anne's Church

I would suggest that it was from this time forward that Lewes began to be poorly favoured by royalty. Given the concessions that came from this defeat (The Mise of Lewes and the Provisions of Oxford), which were subsequent to a mostly unacknowledged and ignored Magna Carta, this stunning revolution must have left a very bad taste in the mouth of the rulers of the time. Lewes has been a haven for free thinkers ever since this fateful battle, with Thomas Paine being a notable example. "Won't be druv!" became an incredibly appropriate old saying for many residents throughout the subsequent ages, right up to this very day... "We will not be driven!" (like cattle).

The Gaol site below St John's sub-Castro was demolished in 1963, and the notorious building at the top of Winterbourne St is now the modern-day prison.

~ CHAPTER 19 ~

CONCLUSION

iven the unlikely chance that all of the connections I have presented here are purely coincidental, we should now take a good look at this probability in light of all of the evidence. It is a simple, unavoidable fact that the geographical situation we find in the Ouse Valley and particularly at Hamsey matches perfectly with all of the descriptions of Geatland in the *Beowulf* text, right down to some extremely unlikely details, including hot springs and dragon legends specific to the area.

If we couple this with the charter descriptions and the historical connections to Hammes, Beow, Old St Peter's, Beornwulf, Wiglaf, Grendel's Gatan, Gote Lane, Middleham, Holt Hill, Harlinges, Halland, Ringmere, Heathfield, Ashdown, Malling Hill, Mt Caburn, Hartfield (Heorot), Beddingham, Denton, Steyning and Bramber, (to name but a few), we can assign a vast array of supporting evidence that occurs in a lone microcosm, and that does not present itself to us anywhere else, not only in Britain, but in the entire world.

Whilst it may be possible to brush off one or two of these connections to the *Beowulf Manuscript* as a coincidence, to dismiss scores of historically documented, related connections that are all found in the same place, would be ridiculous.

It is quite clear that the *Beowulf* legend has its roots firmly in the realms of reality and that Hamsey is the location of Beowulf's death scene. Incredibly, it also seems that somewhere underneath the Hamsey promontory, there lies to this very day, an ancient Roman wall and a treasure vault that may once have been a Roman bathhouse. It seems probable that this vault was entirely emptied by the Geats after the death of Beornwulf; it would be highly unlikely that they would have left anything behind. There is, however, a further possibility for us to now consider. Could this same vault have been repurposed at a later date, by a secretive order in the early 1300s? With a further, deep investigation into this subject, the evidence for this incredible possibility is extremely extensive and will be covered in full in my next book, *Sussex, and the Treasures of the Knights Templar*.

As a final parting thought, I would like to leave you with a short excerpt from the 14th Century Arthurian poem, *Sir Gawain and the Green Knight* by 'The Gawain Poet'. This part of Gawain's journey occurs towards the end of the story and presents us with what should now be some strangely familiar details...

~ Sir Gawain and the Green Knight ~
The Green Chapel

He puts his heels to his horse, and picks up the path;
Goes in beside a grove where the ground is steep,
Rides down the rough slope right to the valley;
And then he looked a little about him-the landscape was wild,
And not a soul to be seen, nor sign of a dwelling,
But <u>high banks on either hand hemmed it about,</u>
With many a ragged rock and rough-hewn crag;
The skies seemed scored by the scowling peaks.
Then he halted his horse, and hoved there a space,
And sought on every side for a sight of the Chapel,
But no such place appeared, which puzzled him sore,
Yet he saw some way off <u>what seemed like a mound,</u>
<u>A hillock high and broad, hard by the water,</u>
<u>Where the stream fell in foam down the face of the steep</u>
<u>And bubbled as if it boiled on its bed below.</u>
The knight urges its horse, and heads for the knoll;
Leaps lightly to earth; loops well the rein
Of his steed to a stout branch, and stations him there.
He strides straight to the mound and strolls all about,
Much wondering what it was, but no whit the wiser;
It had a hole at one end, and on either side,
<u>And was covered with coarse grass in clumps all without,</u>
<u>And hollow all within, like some old cave,</u>
<u>Or a crevice of an old crag he could not discern aright...</u>

AUTHOR ACKNOWLEDGEMENTS

I t has taken a huge amount of effort to produce this book, and I am acutely aware that I could not have completed it without assistance. Here, I would like to take the opportunity to mention the people who most deserve acknowledgment for their essential role in its creation.

Special thanks to Rosa Tomasina for her encouragement, belief and unending support. Your help and kindness have unquestionably contributed to the final production of this book. Without you, I may not have crossed the finishing line. You have been a solid ally and a good friend; offering aid and hope when I really needed it, I will always be grateful for this.

To Jonathan at Country Books, for your tireless work in the production of this beautiful, finished product. Also, for helping me through the publication process and for the critical assistance in obtaining the licenses I required to make this book possible. Without your valuable time and knowledge, once again, I would not have been able to complete this project. Thank you for everything you have done, including the countless minor edits and for helping me through the publication process. Your essential input cannot be underestimated. I am truly grateful for everything you have done.

To the original, unknown author of the Beowulf Manuscript.

If, by some miracle you can learn of this acknowledgement in the afterlife, I would like you to know how important your work has become to the countless historians that succeeded you. Many of us have dedicated much of our lives to your critical text. Without you, our understanding of ancient history, storytelling, and the lives of our ancestors would be severely lacking. This beautiful text of yours, which has now survived over a thousand years since you wrote it, has quite literally changed the face of the world as we know it. Thank you for taking the time to record such a remarkable story and for the incredible puzzle it left us all to decipher, centuries later. You have inspired many generations of historians, teachers and academics, yet sadly, we do not even know your name. Whoever you are, you are a true hero in your own right and many people, including myself, owe you a huge debt of gratitude.

Most importantly to me, I would now like to offer my immeasurable respect and gratitude to one of the most remarkable men to have walked the face of this earth, Beowulf himself. To you, the real-life Beowulf, if it were at all possible, I would like you to know that you lead a life so interesting, so full of adventure and heroism, that even time would not let your name be forgotten. If, as the story of your life implies, you wanted to be remembered above all else, I can confidently inform you that you did achieve this. Thank you for living a most daring, heroic life, and for leaving me with such a fascinating mystery to stumble upon. Your story gave my life meaning when I needed it the most. Whoever you really were, Beowulf, Beornwulf or Ragnar, your bravery long outlived your life. Your deeds have long outlived your flesh. You have become a worthy legend. Thank you for letting me be a small part of it.

Additionally, of course, my personal thanks to God, the creator of everything, who made it all possible in the first place.

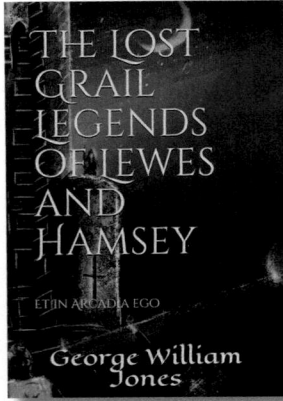

~ FURTHER READING ~

THE LOST GRAIL LEGENDS
OF LEWES AND HAMSEY

By George William Jones

If you would like to know more on this subject, I have published a historical fiction novel covering 2000 years of history and myth in the Ouse Valley, specifically at Hamsey Church.

It is available in Boon Books at the bottom of Lewes High Street, spiral-books.com, or on Amazon worldwide.

Priced at £12.99